Girls Go To Montreal

The

Girls Go To

Montreal

A musical ghost story by Jane Ross Fallon

The Girls Go To Montreal
A Musical Ghost Story

Published by Town Forest Books and Music,
www.townforestbooksandmusic.com

Library of Congress Control Number:
2019900424

Cover Design by Jane Ross Fallon

Fallon, Jane 1953 –
The Girls Go To Montreal/Jane Ross Fallon
ISBN: 978-0-578-44775-9
1. Book 2.Fiction 3.Written Work

About the Music included in

The
Girls Go To Montreal:

Music and Lyrics by Jane Fallon © 2019

*In the story, a ghostly singer helps to unravel
a mystery. The lyrics are in the book and listening
to the songs isn't necessary to understanding
the story.*

*But I hope you will listen!
Songs sung by Jane Ross Fallon with
accompaniment by Doug Kwartler (Hollowbody
Studios) with additional guitar by Kenny Selcer.*

*You can listen to the songs online at
https://soundcloud.com/user9680499/sets/the-girls-go-to-
montreal/s-ShS1k*

*Go to **townforestbooksandmusic.com**
or
www.janefallon.com
for more information on
other formats of this book
or to order a CD*

Acknowledgements

My mother was not a reader, and she never went to college or held a job outside of the home except for a brief turn as an elementary school teacher on a war certificate.

But, somehow, she sensed my hunger for the written word, and every six weeks would take me into the library of the small town of Galt, California where they would let me take out an enormous stack of books. In addition, she pinched the cookie jar a little bit so that I could get my Summer Weekly Reader delivered to the mailbox of our California rural route, and she even let me order some books by mail.

Later, helped by my music teacher, Kent Smith, and with a scholarship from the Soroptimist Club of Baker City, Oregon, I was able to go to Eastern Oregon University where I met incredible teachers who made an impact on me like Hank Larom, Howard Fetz and Mary Jane Loso.

From both sides of my family I inherited an interest in, and a talent for, music. I began writing songs at a young age. However, I did not write any fiction outside of my story songs. Songs came easily and satisfied my creativity. But I always felt that, like many others, I had a novel in me.

I suppose it is only natural for my first novel to be one that includes music. It has been a fun challenge to write this book, figuring out how to incorporate the songs in a way that advanced the plot. For that ability, I again credit those I have mentioned above, as well as the many exceptional university instructors I have taught with, and the many exceptional students who taught me as much as I taught them.

Writing a book with music needs musical helpers. I am surrounded by many talented people, and I am thankful to Doug Kwartler of Hollowbody Studios in Chelmsford, Massachusetts for providing his immense skills towards creating the song tracks, and to the talented Kenny Selcer, for providing a couple of guitar parts for the project.

In addition, I want to thank Carl Jahnle, a personal friend and avid reader, whose career as a high school English teacher made him a perfect choice to proofread my first draft.

I enjoyed creating a work that spanned the country, as has my own life, and that allowed me to combine three things I have always loved: fiction, music, and research.

Chapters

1 Memory Key

2 The Pathway

3 A Garden Party

4 Old Chests and Absent Things

5 They Love Birds There

6 Trading Places

7 Dear Diary

8 The Burnettes

9 Gladys

10 Michael

11 The Girls Go To Montreal

12 Sylvie

13 The Abortion Underground

14 The Rain Has Stopped

15 Digging Up The Past

16 Please Tell My Mother

17 All That Remains

18 Mrs. Bemis Knows

19 Slipping Into Gothic

20 Love Letters

21 Written In Stone

22 Ashes to Ashes

23 Mrs. McNab

24 New Again

Chapter One

Memory Key

It wasn't the same key. It wasn't the same lock. Too many years had gone by, and the old mahogany door that she remembered had been replaced with an insulated reproduction. But somehow, as the key slipped seamlessly into the socket, she was there again. This is the door they came through when the night was black and secret, when her hair was still a wisp of young freedom and he brushed it back with heart-wrenching tenderness. She had looked deeply into his eyes and knew she could trust him.

He had just the beginnings of small lines around his eyes then, but with his bright eyes and dark, raven hair, he could have been just out of college instead of an associate professor. After class, the co-eds gathered at the door, clamoring for attention, looking up with luminous eyes and shy half-smiles vying for attention, a circle of short skirts, long hair, and lipstick around his towering form, elegant in jeans and a tweed jacket, the uniform for the young and upwardly mobile male professor in those days.

"Dr. Metzner," a particularly lovely blonde called out. "Remember you said you would read through my paper with me. It is really important. I need to make sure I am going in the right direction."

He looked at her with a twitch of his handsome lips and a twinkle in his eyes. "Of course, Rebecca. I remember. Come by my office at two."

Linda had watched the dance daily as she left her own classroom across the hall and exited with many fewer fans. After listening to the requisite student excuse or two about the dead grandmother or roommate who took off with the wrong homework, she was able to pass into the hall quietly. What it was that caught his eye she did not know at the time. Later, he said it was because she hadn't tried to catch his. Her pale blue eyes had a preoccupied look, as if her mind was on more important things than the comings and goings of students and professors and their daily flirtations. But, of course, she had noticed. Who wouldn't have?

However, feeling totally out of her element, and knowing her place as an adjunct, she had tried to slip by without acting as if she had noticed.

"Hello!" he said in a brief moment of solitude, as the hallway cleared magically with the beginning of the next period. "Linda Harner. Correct? PhD candidate in English Literature? NYU Grad?"

She looked up shyly. "Well, yes. I am surprised that you know," she said and laughed lightly.

"I read your Master's thesis and believe it or not, I was there when you took your orals."

Her surprise must have been obvious. He laughed. "My good friend is Joshua Bellini. I was visiting and asked to sit in. We are looking to emulate some of their techniques."

"Dr. Bellini! He was my advisor!"

"Yes" he said with a smile. "I know. He asked me to keep on eye on you, but you seem to be doing a pretty good job for yourself. I have been remiss in my duty. Coffee?"

She nodded, and they adjourned to a small cafe just a short walk away on the outskirts of campus, a place where the students never went and the professors could be free to unwind away from their scrutiny.

Those coffee dates became regular occurrences and transformed into wine and cheese afternoons and then into bistro evenings. They led, finally, to the upstairs bedroom of the old Victorian two-story house. It was here they hatched their plans. It was here he cradled her 26-year-old head in his 38-year-old arms and whispered her future into her ear.

As she slipped that key into the socket, this is what surrounded her. *I suppose that is why I came back.*

Even though they had spent only six months here after they had married, before moving to Pennsylvania, this is where she most felt alive. It is where she felt so totally connected to him. It is where her life began in a way she had never imagined. In his death, it is where she felt closest to him.

The inside of the house was very different than it had been, as one might expect. Forty years and several residents had decorated it in a much different manner, and the blue floral wallpaper and dark wood paneling had been exchanged for the muted paints favored by the contemporary era. But the chandeliers were still there, and the basic layout remained as if she had walked away yesterday.

As she drank it all in, her phone rang. Startled from her reverie, she pulled it out of her purse. "Hello?"

"Linda? This is Cassie. Is everything ok? Do you need any help moving in?"

Cassie Milquist was her realtor. "No, thanks anyway. I have a moving company on its way. The house looks great. Nice. Clean. I can't wait to explore it."

"Well, if you need anything, let me know."

"Of course."

She clicked off her phone and, looking around with a deep sigh, said aloud, "What I need is no longer here. What I need is Alex, and he is gone."

She spent the night in a Holiday Inn that had not been there when she had left the area and the next day, after the movers had filled the house with her belongings, she moved into this home of her heart, this structure of memory and, as she traced her hand over the deep, mahogany stair rail, she felt one small tear slip from her pale blue eyes. She said to herself, "I will be happy here. I will be happy here. I will remember for both of us."

She used to wear silk to bed. Only silk. Long silk, swirling around her ankles, just bare enough to reveal her sculpted neck bone and a hint of cleavage, but with enough sensible coverage to be comfortable. Alex loved her in silk. Since he died, she had switched to cotton: eyelet for summer, flannel for winter. That first night in her new home she wore flannel. The late summer evenings were cool.

It wasn't the same bed. She was glad for that. She had kept a lot of the furniture - some had been in this house when Alex had bought it and had been there for years. When they moved from Greenbriar, they had exchanged that old four-poster in heavy oak for a modern king-sized bed in light wood. But, she had not brought that with her. She sold the bed she had shared with Alex and bought a double bed that would not let her miss the warmth of his body, hoping that the size constraints would also constrain the grief.

Like Hamlet, she wondered what dreams might come. But whether it was sheer will or just the result of extreme exhaustion, she fell into a deep sleep as soon as her head hit the pillow and woke with the confusion one gets when startled from deepest reverie to a place that is strange and yet familiar. The sun came in the same old windows, painting her eyes in the same place it had painted them back then, but the draperies were different. As she rose, her feet traveled the same floors, only the old-fashioned carpet had been stripped away to reveal the original hardwood. As she took her first morning breath, the rose-scented breeze greeted her in the same way it had when her young life was filled with love, happiness, and hope for the future.

She had almost finished unpacking when the doorbell rang.

"Maureen!" That round, sweet face with crinkly blown eyes was unmistakable. "How did you know I was here?"

"Oh, there are no secrets in Greenbriar!" She winked. "My good friend is Cassie Milquist. I coaxed it out of her."

"Well, I have no problem with that. It is so nice to see you. How long has it been? Maybe ten years ago at Dean Johnson's retirement?"

"Yes, I think so. You had to come alone because Alex was otherwise indisposed. I am sorry about that. I missed the last chance I might have had to see him." Her eyes filled with a soft look of sympathy. "I am sorry Linda. Did he linger?"

"No, one day he just clutched his heart and dropped to the floor. I guess there are worse ways to go."

Several cups of tea and years worth of gossip and catching up later, Maureen stood and collected her things.

"Yikes! Where does the time go? Look, we will get together again. I have a whole list of things

I intend to make you be involved in."

She walked through the door, and then turned briefly and smiled. "I am glad you are back, Linda. Welcome home."

That night was not quite as restful as the previous one. With the bulk of the moving-in behind her, and so many memories gathering around her, she guessed it was too much to ask that she spend another dreamless night. For some unknown reason she dreamed about bees. She saw trees and a well. And meadows. And there was a radio playing. She thought it was a radio. She heard music. Haunting music. Lovely, melancholy music.

She woke with it in her head and throughout the day it would come back. A snippet here, a word there. She would dismiss it, but it wouldn't let go. It became stronger that night. The voice had a sweet poignancy and the words became more clear.

Quickly, Linda jumped out of bed and went to the nearby desk. She scribbled madly on the white notepad she left there for whenever the muse might strike her. Furiously she wrote and then, finally spent, collapsed into a black, uninterrupted sleep.

She woke late to sun streaming into the window. It was late. She went to her desk to read that fierce scribbling, those words that had come to her in a dream.

It took a few days for her to completely transcribe them, and as the words began to make sense, she heard the melody as well. It was a song.

An entire song.

When a song comes out of nowhere
And lingers in your mind
It is talking to the future
About the past you've left behind.
And sometimes it will seem
Like it isn't very clear
When a song comes out of nowhere.
You have brought a key
And it has turned the lock,
But remember that real time
Doesn't live inside a clock.
Just believe your eyes,
Don't question what you hear
When a song comes out of nowhere.
Out of nowhere like the wind,
Out of nowhere like a cloud,
A simple feeling taking flight from nowhere.
When a song comes out of nowhere
It will haunt you like a ghost,
And it will make you question
The things you love the most.
It will set on fire
Much that you hold dear,
When a song comes out of nowhere.
In the grass down by the river

Is a secret all alone
On a path that no one travels
Buried 'neath a stone.
You can uncover truth
By facing all your fears
When a song comes out of nowhere.
When a song comes out of nowhere.
When a song comes out of nowhere.

Linda was perplexed. This wasn't like the usual poetry that came to her in her dreams. This was something totally different.

The day went by quickly as she unpacked and put things in place, but she was somewhat haunted by the words she had written down that morning. Something nagged at her all day. As she tried to read, it kept coming into her mind unbidden. As she wiped dishes and trimmed plants, as she swept the crumbs and vacuumed the rug, it pulled at her. Then a memory came.

Linda. Alex's voice coaxed her. Come on. Put away the papers. You will have plenty of time to grade those.

She pushed his hands away. Alex, I have midterms to grade too.

You'll have time. I will take you to dinner. Meanwhile, it is a beautiful day. Take a little walk with me.

Yes, it was a beautiful day, and Alex's eyes were irresistible. He took her hand and said, Let's sneak off. Get out of this stuffy office. I want to take you to my special place.

He drove them to his house. I bought this house right after I got hired at Greenbriar. There is something I want to show you - something out back.

They walked toward a gap between the dark oaks and then down to a narrow path that curved softly towards a river. He led her to a shadowy outcropping on a hill overlooking the small valley.

My cave, he smiled. Merlin's nest. They laughed. He pointed to a grassy promontory. I would always come here when I wanted to get away. I swore it was the place where I would someday be buried.

He drew her down into the shadows. Marry me Linda. He stroked her cheek and then her hair and they lay down in the soft dew. She said, yes.

She shook her head to dismiss the images and finally she gave in to something else that had been nagging at her persistently. She went to the desk and pulled out her transcription of the song she had heard in the nighttime. The words began to mean something. *I have been there.* In her memory she saw it all: the path, the grass, the river.

But the song mentions something buried beneath a stone. A gravestone?

There were no gravestones there the day I threw back my head and let him kiss my neck.

When I said yes.

Chapter Two

The Pathway

The way between the trees was greatly overgrown, and she had to push back the branches as she walked along. The narrow path along the river had not changed at all, and she gradually made her way up into the shadowy outcropping. It was much as she had remembered it, but this time she looked at it with new eyes.

Linda searched for those words she had heard in the song. She looked for the gravestone. There it was, in the cradle of memory, gray and silent.

She approached it with breath held and knees trembling. In that place where her life had changed, where her love had lived, was this mystery grave. Or so it appeared to be. It was a smooth, gray granite stone, arched as gravestones often are. It was smaller than most gravestones however, and there was a definite etching: a small flower in middle. That was all.

She stared at the scene in mild wonder. If she had stumbled on this stone on her own, if she hadn't been led there by a song that told her to look for it, would she have noticed it? Would she have thought it was a gravestone?

She walked back in silence.

For many days after that she was drawn to the grass promontory overlooking the river. She would sit by the stone and ask for it to talk to her. *Who are you? What do you want? Did you sing to me?* And, as the sky dimmed and the trees turned amber, she got no answers.

Until one night.

She dressed again in warm cotton flannel to keep her comfortable throughout the night and slipped reluctantly into bed. She tried to sleep, but sleep would not come; she lay instead with her eyes open and her ears ready. *Come to me. I know you are there.*

And the music came. That voice so sweet and poignant. And then, she saw a shape. It was just a shape, somewhat misty and undefined. It played and sang as if Linda were not there. It wasn't the same song as before, and she didn't need to write it down. It burned itself into her brain:

It was hidden in the attic and
He just shrugged his shoulders.
There is nothing in that chest
That is important to me.
Old transcripts, tax returns, recommendations,
Things you gotta keep but
No one needs really needs to see.
So it stayed there in the attic
All of your life together
And you moved it with you when he died.
You always felt someday when you were ready
You would take a look, a look inside.
Something's missing from
The papers in the big brown chest,
You should be finding something
That you do not see.
You always thought you were the one
Who knew him best,
But I guess you had better go and ask Marie.
Take a look in the chest up there in the attic
And you'll find things that just aren't right.
You might discover that
He's not the man you thought
You knew when you
Went to sleep last night.
The chest is filled and yet it is empty

—

Of some things that you might expect to find.
Those kinds of possessions you keep forever
If you wanna leave a part of yourself behind.
Something's missing from the papers
In the big brown chest
You should be finding something
that you do not see.
You always thought you were the one
Who knew him best
But I guess you had better
Go and ask Marie.

For days, this song circled inside of her head. Who is the "he" in this song? What chest is she referring to? Does this have something to do with the gravestone?

Chapter Three

A Garden Party

No of course not. Alex laughed. It was just a joke. I certainly don't want to be buried out there on the promontory.

He seemed nervous as he quickly dried the evening's dishes.

In fact, I have been meaning to talk to you. I have

decided to take a position at the University of Pennsylvania. I think I have done all I can here. It is time for me to move on.

She didn't even try to hide her shock. Just like that? You might have discussed this with me.

It is best for you. You finish up your PhD next month and there is nothing for you here. There are several colleges in the Pennsylvania region where you should have a good chance of getting an assistant professorship - I have already put in a good word for you with some people I know.

He paused and stared out of the window. Then he turned and flashed that irresistible smile at her. Cupping her face in his hands, he looked earnestly into her eyes.

Believe me. This is best for you and it is best for me. I have been here too long. I am tired of the town, tired of the people, tired of the university. It is time for a change.

"Garden Party?" she said to Maureen. "You want me to host a garden party?"

"Why not. You have a big beautiful home and a garden. What else do you need? It will be great way to meet people in the neighborhood."

"But I have barely had time to settle in!"

Linda laughed.

"I will help," she said. "We will call Branoza's. They will deliver some nice cafe tables and chairs for the outside patio. Julie Masters can cater. She does wonderful buffets. All you have to do is dress nice and smile."

Reunions are always a bit surreal. Linda stood, smiling with a forced cheerfulness, in that garden that was at once the same and yet so different as faces she somewhat recognized floated by. They had the advantage. They knew that her strange face was the older version of the Linda they had known. She, on the other hand, had to process the features from a different time, putting names to those that looked familiar.

Maureen was at her side, however.

"Helen!" she cried, as a plump, shorthaired woman approached with a smile.

"Helen Jenkins! So glad you could make it."

Linda took her cue. Her mouth said, "Yes, Helen, so nice to see you. You look wonderful!" while her brain said, "Wow, I would not have recognized you at all."

The rest of the greetings happened in the same way, and she gave Maureen a thankful look.

The last person to come through the door was easily recognizable, however. It wasn't that she hadn't changed, she was older like everyone else, but that special look she had always possessed was still there. Her perpetual air of calm, kind eyes, and competent "may I help you" smile had not gone away.

"Mrs. Bemis!" Linda cried and gave her a hug. "I am so glad that you are still in Greenbriar. You totally saved my first year here."

Georgia Bemis had been the department secretary for what had seemed forever. She shuffled schedules, took phone calls, arranged meetings and most of all, provided a shoulder to cry on. They all knew that they could vent to Mrs. Bemis and it wouldn't go any further.

"Yes, I don't know where else I would go," she laughed. "They finally made me retire last year."

"You stayed on that long!" Linda was really not surprised. Sitting at the desk outside of the Dean's office had just been where Mrs. Bemis had belonged.

"Yes, my whole life has been here. 50 years at the school."

"You were hired the same year as Alex I believe?"

She smiled. "Yes we were neophytes together. He was the one I could secretly roll my eyes at when politics went over the top.

"Dashing, charming Alex." Her eyes became a little misty. "How the girls loved him. I could have fallen for him myself if I hadn't already met Bill – and of course, I knew what a rascal he was."

She laughed. "But then he met you and settled

right down. You were the best thing that happened to Alex Metzner."

"Well, I am glad you were taken. Alex may never have been able to pass you up," Linda smiled. "Yes, I know about how the girls gathered round. But that is pretty typical for the young, handsome professors." She winked. "Unless, there's something I don't know?"

She had meant it as a joke, but Mrs. Bemis didn't respond right away. She hesitated for just an instance before commenting as she laughed, "Oh, I am sure you knew him better than anyone else ever did."

As the sun began to set, the clatter of dishes and the folding of chairs mixed with the "goodbyes" and the "thankyous." "So nice to see you." "Glad you are back." "I will be in touch."

When at last it was just herself and Maureen, Linda was pretty weary.

"Was it too much?"

"No, I am glad you made me do it. I might have hidden in this house for months before venturing forth. It is nice to find that so many people I knew stayed here."

"Greenbriar attracts those types. It is a university where a few come to start and then move on, like you and Alex, but most come to stay."

"It was especially nice to see Mrs. Bemis. When I think of the Liberal Arts Department at Greenbriar, I think of Mrs. Bemis. Deans came and went, professors were born and died, but Mrs. Bemis was always there. I remember how she helped me through that scheduling mess when Dr. Lammert tried to bury my course in 8 a.m. obscurity. No one wants to study anything, much less Intro to Lit, at 8 in the morning."

"Yes," Maureen said. "There was no Department Head at Greenbriar who could resist Georgia." She chuckled. "I think it was because she knew where all of the bodies were buried."

Something twitched in Linda's chest. She felt that her eyes must have indicated her distress.

"Oh Linda. I am so sorry. So soon after Alex's death. What a clumsy thing for me to say."

"No," she recovered. "That's ok. It isn't what you think. I have some processing to do, but soon, there is something I want to tell you – at the right time."

Chapter Four

Old Chests and Absent Things

Simplicity is making the journey of this life with just baggage enough Alex said with a final "umpff" as he dropped his small chest onto the bed.

Ok, ok, don't go quoting Thoreau on me, she said. I don't do American Lit.

Not Thoreau. A fellow named Charles Dudley Smith. A simple journalist whose pithy sayings often get attributed to other people.

Well, whoever said it, is this pithy comment relating to the fact that I have just carried up four suitcases and four boxes of personal items and all you have brought is one suitcase, a garment bag and that chest?

Let's see, he reflected. Three jackets. Three white shirts. Two pairs of trousers. Black and gray for work. Oh, and a collection of zany ties. No one notices a man's dress uniform, so just add a different tie and it's a different uniform every day. For leisure, two pairs of jeans, one pair of khakis, two canvas shirts. Throw it all together with a sweater, a vest, a parka, and assorted undergarments, and what else does a man need?

Men are fortunate. If a woman shows up in the same dress two days in a row, the gossips would be buzzing. Hmm. Where did she sleep last night, the tongues would flap and the eyes would roll. And they would said "Hello", with a knowing smile on their sickly faces and you would want to slap them, but you can't because that's not polite. But, aside from that, a woman just needs more. Dressy dresses, sporty skirts, pants and jackets for those authoritarian days. And don't even talk outerwear to me. A woman needs a pea coat for those jean days but camel hair for dress trousers. Then, there is the parka for the truly cold weather - wait, two parkas: one for trousers and one long enough to cover the skirt. Which brings me to the topic of sweaters. How do men get away with wearing the same gray sweater? Sometimes women need a zipped collar pullover, another day might warrant a turtleneck, while the next will require a scooped neck.

Well, he said. I salute you. To quote your beloved Shakespeare, the apparel oft proclaims the man; however I prefer Mark Twain. Clothes make the man. Naked people have little or no influence in society. So I will let you make our mark on society and I will go about as the underdressed professor.

He set down his last item of baggage. Then he removed the chest from the bed and looked around. Given all of your possessions, I guess my chest of assorted professional memorabilia should be put in the attic.

Then he gave her a once over, flashed that irresistible smile and, as he pulled their T-shirts and jeans off, he said right now I would prefer us to have very little influence on society. It is time to inaugurate our new home.

She thought about the day that they had moved in and compared it to this new moving day. Alex had possessed few things beside books and his wooden chest.

"A chest of assorted professional memorabilia,"

he had called it.

She suddenly recalled a line she had heard in the last song: "*the chest is filled and yet it is empty.*"

It had been years since Linda had looked into that chest. She had never examined it closely, and Alex had never seemed too interested in it. She just had figured it was his way of keeping tabs on old records and transcripts - maybe some letters or notes.

She had brought it with her and stowed it in the attic where it had lived before. It had not seemed important enough at the time to go through it, but it would have hurt her to get rid of it.

Linda sat on the floor of the attic and carefully opened the bronze latch. The contents were what she expected to find. There were several file folders that were neatly labeled: Transcripts, Recommendations, Personal Correspondence, Birth Certificate, Passport, and Miscellaneous.

She carefully sorted through it all and gained no new insights. There was no new information about Alex.

Yes, she thought, it contains so very little. Here were the remnants of a professional, adult life, but what was missing seemed significant. How little she knew about Alex's background. He had hesitated to talk about it. He had been an orphan and spent his formative years in foster homes in Ridgefield, Washington, where he had been a star basketball player and stellar student. He had come with her to her high school reunions but had shown no interest in his own. "There is nothing to go back to - no one to go back to," he always said with a shrug of his shoulders.

The transcripts were there, the A's on the report cards and the acceptance to Yale. He had glowing recommendations from his teachers and some personal correspondence from them while he was at Yale.

But something was missing. There were no yearbooks, no newspaper clippings, and no evidence of his athletic glory. There was nothing truly personal in this box. He hadn't really talked about that aspect of his life, so perhaps it hadn't mattered to him. But, still it seemed odd that he had kept nothing from his high school days, none of the kind of memorabilia from a time that most want to hold on to.

She thought about her own records. She didn't keep them in a wooden box with a bronze latch, but had transferred them from a metal file cabinet to a plastic storage box. Her entire life was in there, including all her high school yearbooks and clippings from the hometown newspaper when she had made honor roll. Sure, she had her transcripts and recommendations as well, even old papers from her college days. But her early life was there as well. That was what was missing from his box.

She went downstairs slowly and thoughtfully

and took out the journal where she had scratched down the lyrics that she had heard the night before. *Something's missing from the papers in the big brown chest. I guess you better go and ask Marie.*

Marie. That had caught her attention immediately. She had wondered who this Marie person was.

The garden party, with its emotional turmoil of meeting and greeting old friends, had drained whatever strength she had left and she slept soundly. A sunny breeze and the sound of birds woke her as it had during that summer Alex and she had spent here and, for a moment, she was transported. She expected a young Alex to walk through the door, having risen early as he was wont to do, and say, "Wake up sleepy head - the day's a-wastin' and you don't need any beauty sleep."

But that strange sensation didn't last long. She went into the shower and scrubbed herself hard with the blissfully hot water. When she came out, the past was gone and the present had returned. Throughout the day, she went about making the house her own, positioning pictures and stacking clothing.

She really felt that she could leave it alone. It had just been a dream - there was nothing to it. But throughout the day, she seemed to hear the voice.

That night sleep did not come so easily and she would wake, sure she heard the tune and almost certain she saw a shape in the corner.

No, this isn't going away, she thought. Only

what we don't know can harm us, she thought. So, the researcher in her began to urge the inevitable. Maybe it was because she was back at her old post-grad stomping grounds, but she had an urge to head for the library. However, she had learned that times had changed since her college days and that her best bet would be the Internet.

She trudged up to the attic once more, and this time she looked carefully through Alex's correspondence. Most of the letters were from Alex's teachers or from places he had studied or taught. However, one brief message stood out. It was from a friend.

"Dear Alex. I take it that you are enjoying your time at Yale since we haven't seen or heard from you since. I can understand. You don't have much to come home to. The basketball team hasn't been the same since you left, and we can't seem to win anything. Coach Swenson has moved on and the new guy has some promise, but we don't have anyone of your ability at point. I just got accepted to Oregon State and am looking forward to that. Anyway, if you get a chance let us all know how you are doing. Oh, and we are having a memorial for Larry on the anniversary of the accident. June 4th.

If you think you could make it, everyonewould love to see you. Regards, Billy Preston."

Billy Preston and somebody named Larry

seemed like a good enough starting place.

Her cellphone was ringing when she got back down to the kitchen. "Hello?" she said, not sure who might be calling her at this new location.

"Mrs. Metzner?"

"Yes, this is Mrs. Metzner."

"This is Telecom Services. You called about getting cable and Internet service set up in your house?"

"Oh, yes. I am glad you called. I will be available all this week. If you could let me know when you can send someone over?"

By Wednesday it was all set up. The cable was connected and the WIFI was sending a strong signal to the laptop computer that she had set up in the small office room that was just off of the kitchen.

On Thursday morning, she took her coffee to her desk and logged in. She had an obvious starting place - Facebook. There was only one high school in Ridgefield, so she searched for a Facebook page for Ridgefield High School in Ridgefield, WA. Yes, it had one - an open group. She searched through the list of those who had joined the group and it was almost too easy. William Preston.

She hesitated a moment before she clicked "message," but she knew she had to follow through on this.

"Hello Bill? Is this the Billy Preston who played on the basketball team with Alex Metzner? This is his wife, Linda. I would love to speak with you. If you would prefer, you can email me at l.metzner@telecom.net."

She pushed the send arrow and sat back with a sigh. *I will just wait to see how this plays out.* She went into the garden to pull a few weeds and scope out where she might want to put in an herb patch. When she came back, she sat down at the laptop and took a deep breath. Right there was a little notification that she had a message. "Yes, this is Billy Preston, and I did know your husband. No one has heard from him since he left town. The local newspaper reported that he had graduated from Yale with his PhD, and that was the last thing we heard. Is he still around? I am so glad you got in touch. Is it ok if we talk by phone? I don't do too much of this Internet stuff."

She assured him that was fine and gave him her number. That afternoon she received the call. After catching him up on Alex's life and informing him of his death, she jumped right in since she didn't couldn't see any other way to begin.

"Billy, I realized I don't have any papers or pictures from Alex's high school years and wondered if you might have anything you could send me?"

"Sure, I will copy off some pictures from my junior yearbook. Alex was a senior then, and it is filled with pictures of him. Captain of the basketball team, King of the Prom, participant in many organizations. You can't miss him. What is your

---

address?"

She waited in anticipation, hoping that Billy would fulfill that promise. Meanwhile, she took a few walks back to the hidden meadow and sat and reflected about all that was being thrown at her. What does it all mean? *Is something or somebody really buried out here? What does that have to do with Alex?*

The package arrived in the mail a week later. Billy had been true to his word and copied many pages from the yearbook. But as much as Linda studied the prints, she found it hard to recognize Alex. *Had he changed that much?* She had met him when he was 35, but 17 years should not have made much of a difference. The hair color was the same. The height and the build were similar. Maybe it was the grainy reproduction. The yearbook had not been in great shape obviously, and the copies reflected that.

Just as she was about to put the pictures down in disappointment, she saw one more at the bottom of the box. It was a reprint of a yearbook photo page. She scanned quickly for Alex's picture and her eyes stopped on a photo that was just above his. The name read "Larry Martin", and he was a dead ringer for her husband.

She was shaken, but determined. *What had the song said? "Remember that real time doesn't live inside a clock?" And the line that had said, "you always thought you were the one who knew him best"?*

She knew now that she was meant to continue looking into this. The watery vision and crystal clear voice were there to tell her something. She could not turn her back on this journey.

The next morning she logged back on to the Internet, and this time she had a fierce desire to find out what this was all about. Could the yearbook have made a mistake? She thought about going back to Billy Preston, but it wasn't something that could be talked about on the phone and Billy might find it too confusing. Plus, she wasn't ready to talk about this until she knew more.

Ridgefield High School had a great website, but she couldn't find much there. And so, she went to a much better source, The Ridgefield County Library, and struck gold. She clicked the link to a site called Discover Ridgefield, Washington. It was an historical newspaper archive site. In the database were over 2.3 million old newspaper articles that mentioned 5.6 billion people! The search engine was very advanced. Her search was fruitful. Alex Metzner turned up in many articles. He had indeed been a stand out. But Larry Martin was harder. All she found was that he was in the graduating class of 1954.

But she wasn't ready for what she found next. The story had made the front page.

"Local Teenager Is Killed In Fiery Crash." She scanned the article quickly:

—

"A body found in a one-car collision on Rt. 503, north of Chelatchie, has been identified as Larry Martin, a senior at Ridgefield High School. The car was completely in flames by the time police and firefighters arrived. It is believed that the driver was killed upon impact. The body was burned beyond recognition. However, identification was made by the dog tags that the young man always wore. They had belonged to his uncle and godfather who had been killed in France. Police are still investigating the crash, but it is believed that his Chevrolet Corvette spun out of control to avoid a collision with a lumber truck and crashed into a stand of trees before overturning. Larry had just received his new car as a graduation present."

A further search came up with an obituary:

Lawrence Kenneth Martin, 18, was killed in a car crash on Saturday, June 4th. The funeral services will be held at St. Mary's Church in Ridgefield, and he will be buried at the St. Mary's Cemetery in the family plot. Larry Martin was a senior at Ridgefield High School. He leaves behind his father, John, and his mother Alice, as well as a younger sister, Marie. Donations to the Larry Martin scholarship fund may be made instead of flowers. Contact Ridgefield High School for details.

It took a while for this to sink it. She made some tea, and went out to the garden to sit for awhile.

—

So, Larry Martin, who looks like my husband, was killed in a car crash in 1954, shortly after graduation. Alex Metzner, who shows up in so many articles in college, just goes off to Yale and is never heard from again. But through the entire reverie, there is something that overshadows it all. Marie. Larry had a younger sister named Marie. *Ask Marie.*

She forced herself to go back to the laptop, and back to the Ridgefield High Facebook page, where she found a Marie Martin Alcott. A quick search on www.whitepages.com yielded the following: Marie Martin Alcott, 69. 193 Wilmington Way, Ridgefield, WA.

She had just settled in to this new place, but she knew what she had to do. She had to go to Washington.

Chapter Five

They Love Birds There

Ridgefield? Alex said with a slight pursing of his lower lip and a shrug of his shoulders. It's a great place if you like dull. Or birds. They love birds in Ridgefield. He turned away from her and ran a comb through his hair. He did look very urbane in his gray flannels and tweed coat. With his head down, he slipped his keys into his pocket and said quietly, there is nothing for me in Ridgefield.

The city of Portland, Oregon is nestled between the ocean and the mountains and imbued with a college town vibe; it begs to be walked, shopped, and dined. Linda had made several trips there to conferences during her academic career and had thought it odd that Alex always had excuses for not joining her. However, she had finally just chalked it up to his having an anathema for the Pacific Northwest in general, the place where he had no family and nothing to go back to. However, now she was now beginning to question her hypothesis.

She had called Marie before she left the East Coast. "Is this Marie Martin Alcott?" she asked.

"Yes, speaking."

"Well, this may seem like a bolt out of the blue, but my name is Linda Metzner. I believe that my husband, Alex Metzner, was a friend of your brother Larry."

"Alex! Oh my. We haven't heard from him since he left Ridgefield years ago, right after high school. I always wondered what happened to him."

"I am sorry to say that he has passed away. I won't say anymore right now. I would like to be able to talk about Alex in person. There is much I don't know about his early life.

"I am heading to Portland for a conference *(so I lied - it seemed much better than admitting that I was sleuthing)* and would love to drive up to Ridgefield to meet you. I can tell you more then."

"Why that would be fine," she replied. When

would you be coming?"

Linda told her she would be there on the following week, having already checked the flight schedules and reserved tickets. She packed a small carryon with clothing and her head with questions. An overnight at the airport would give her time to prepare herself.

The next day, after a sleepless night at the Shilo Inn, she shuttled back to the terminal and rented a car for the brief drive across the Columbia River and into the small town of Ridgefield.

Just 10 minutes and three rotaries off the interstate, Ridgefield appeared like Brigadoon, a town just barely changed by time. She took a quick breather at the little park that greeted her as she ran out of road in the town center. A concrete stage with a curved bronze arch overhead was the focal point, but the natural beauty of the Ridgefield National Wildlife refuge provided a backdrop. She quickly read the information about the park after she used the restrooms. "Established in 1965". That was after Alex had left the town. *But I would bet the farm, as the saying goes, that the high school students in the town had made use of it in its unofficial state.*

As she looked down the Main Street, a slight smile came to her lips when she saw the small tapestries that decorated the light poles. *Birds*. Welcome to Ridgefield.

She sat on a bench and contemplated it all.

———

Linda had been raised in the city, in a big suburb outside New Jersey. For a moment she tried to understand what it might mean to be raised in such a small town. One benefit might be the homey feeling - one detriment might be the homey feeling! She had a hard time understanding what it felt like to grow up where everyone knows everyone else's business, where those who are different stand out so strongly and it isn't easy to just walk invisibly. That had been her as a child. She had been shy. She had her set of friends, but for most of the time she just blended in. She did well in school, but hadn't stood out. She looked like everyone else, but was neither extra pretty nor homely. *I didn't excel at anything but never got in trouble either. What impact might all the microscopic attention have on a child?*

Finally, she wandered through the side streets of small, neat homes until she found the address she was given, and rang the bell. A tall and trim lady, dressed elegantly in white slacks and a purple short-sleeved sweater greeted her at the door.

"Marie?" she asked.

"Yes, Linda? Come in."

They settled on the settee in the garden room. She offered Linda tea, and without being asked, began the conversation.

"So tell me about Alex. I was only ten when he left Ridgefield, but remember him so well. He was my brother Larry's best friend. Even though he was everything my brother Larry could never

---

be, there was something that drew the two of them together."

Her curiosity aroused, Linda encouraged Marie to talk. "This is so interesting. Let me give you the rudiments of what Alex was up to after he left here. Then, I would like you to just tell me everything you remember."

Linda briefly went through Alex's professional career and then their marriage, speaking quietly and with composure, despite an underlying anxiety.

"It was a fine, if predictable life I guess. Both of us were only-children and, ironically, we couldn't have children of our own. My parents died about 15 years ago and, since then, it was just the two of us. Alex worked in an emeritus capacity at the university, and I had just retired when he had his stroke. He mentioned he was from Ridgefield - and that they loved birds here - otherwise, he never talked much about his past. It was as if it was painful for him. It was only in going through some of his things that I ran across the reference to your brother." *Not a total lie this time - I had read about Larry. I just didn't have a clue who he was until I had talked to Billy.*

"I am so glad that Alex had such a fine and distinguished career. He certainly deserved it. He is still a bit of a legend around here. His basketball and academic abilities drew a great deal of attention to Ridgefield."

She poured us another cup of tea. "So, you would just like me to tell you what I remember?"

Linda nodded. She hoped she remained composed despite her beating heart.

"I was just in grade school when Alex started coming to the house. He and Larry were on the junior varsity basketball team then. Alex was also a whiz at the language and used to help Larry with his English papers. Even when Alex made the varsity basketball team and Larry didn't, they stayed friends.

"My Dad and Mom loved Alex. They felt he was a good influence on Larry, who was a bit of an underachiever. And I think that our home gave Alex a bit of a place to belong. He had been orphaned you know?"

"Yes, he told me that. And that he had spent his young life in a series of foster homes."

"That's true. However, he might not have told you that his mother was the local prostitute and he really didn't know who his dad was, but she used to say it was Bob Metzner. He died in jail, but she had that name put on the birth certificate. She died when he was six and county services stepped forward; he spent the rest of the formative years in foster care. I don't know why no one stepped forward to adopt him - maybe because of his mother's reputation. People can be mean spirited that way. Even his foster homes let him down as, one by one, they dissolved through divorce or disinterest.

"During his senior year of high school he lived with us, and we got to live vicariously through his achievements. My dad was very proud of him. You would have thought he was his own son."

"How did Larry feel about that?" Linda asked.

She smiled a little ruefully. "Well, I was young as I said, but I remember times that Larry would leave the table and go pound a ball against a wall really hard while my dad would talk to Alex about his college prospects. You see, Dad was a self-made man, and he always regretted that he hadn't received an Ivy League education. It was what he wanted for Larry. However, I think he began to realize that Larry just didn't have the mental ability to get into a school like that. Alex, on the other hand, was naturally bright. He made all A's and was Valedictorian. You must know that though?"

Linda nodded, but didn't say anything. She just wanted her to talk.

"I remember a little tenseness those last few months before Larry and Alex were set to graduate. Alex seemed eager to move on to his new life. He had organized his important papers into a small boxand packed a simple suitcase of meager belongings. I remember Larry giving him advice.

———

'You don't need a lot of variety in clothes Alex. Have fewer things, but make sure they are all high quality.' "

Linda stiffened at that but kept her smile fixed on Marie as she spoke.

"Graduation was splendid. Alex shone giving his speech. Larry was just another graduate, but seemed to be happy for his friend. We had a big party here and Dad couldn't make enough of Alex." She paused and looked slightly wistful. "I wore a beautiful pink dress with white eyelet." She laughed. "Amazing that I still remember that."

Linda felt it might be time to give her a little nudge.

"So, Alex mentioned in some correspondence he left behind that Larry died young? What happened?"

A sigh as deep as any well escaped from her thin frame. "Well, for one thing, that was the beginning of the end for my family. It was two days after graduation. Dad had given Larry a Corvette for a graduation present." She gave Linda a sidelong glance. "As much as Dad might have been disappointed in Larry's academic ability, he still spoiled him. That night, he and Alex headed out to Yale Lake. They joked that it would be a good way to get Alex ready for Yale University. Dad advised them about driving the road and said it was very twisty and that they should definitely leave to come back before dark.

"Well, dark came and there was no sign of them. By eleven that night, Dad was ready to head out searching for them when he got the call. Larry's car had been found twisted into an unrecognizable shape near a horseshoe curve. It was totally destroyed by fire and there were the remains of one body. They brought the remains into the morgue and it was obviously Larry. What was left of his clothing that was able to survive the fire was unmistakably his: his treasured belt buckle (one of the few things he had ever won - in a shooting contest with the rifle team), one leather shoe, and most importantly, my uncle Frank's dog tags. Uncle Frank and been killed in WWII and dad gave his dog tags to Larry. Larry never took them off. But they only found one body. Alex was nowhere to be found."

Linda hesitated to ask what seemed a foolish question. "Alex disappeared? Were they so sure it was Larry then? Did they check dental records or anything like that?"

She looked at her puzzled. "I guess that wouldn't have occurred to anyone. It was Larry's car and his personal possessions. Plus, we received a letter from Alex shortly after that. He claimed that he had not driven home with Larry that night. He had decided to stay at a friend's house instead.

"He said he urged Larry to do the same, but Larry had said Dad would kill him if he didn't come home.

"Alex wrote that he was filled with shame and immense sorrow that he had let Larry down. Had he been there, he wrote, Larry wouldn't have gone so fast around those tricky curves. You know, I still have that letter. I pulled it out for you."

Marie handed Linda a typed letter that pretty much related what Marie had just told her. "I can't bear this. After all your family has done for me, I should not have been so selfish. I have made arrangements to leave for Yale, and I don't intend to come back. Please don't come looking for me. Like Larry, let me be dead to you. Put a flower on his grave for me, Alex."

There was no signature, just a typed name.

"So, Alex took off before even coming back? How was it he had his things with him?"

"We aren't sure about that. We don't even know how he got himself back from the Lake. The friend he stayed with perhaps. But when we went up to his room, it was clean. He had obviously taken his things before he and Larry went on that drive."

We both sat in silence for a few moments. Then Linda asked her, "What about Larry's things? Was anything missing?"

"Well, that is odd that you mention it. Mom and Dad couldn't bear to go into Larry's room for the longest time. Finally they hired a cleaning company to just come in and take away everything. "The only reason I have these yearbooks, with the letter tucked inside, is that they were stored in the family library. I don't have anything else of Larry's except some photos that I had saved myself."

After a short pause, she said. "I am surprised that Alex never told you about that night. About him and Larry. It seems like he would have wanted you to know."

"It would seem so," Linda said. "But I guess some pain is so difficult it can't be remembered. Perhaps Alex just wanted to move on and block it all out. Thanks for talking with me. But before I leave - I have an early flight back to Boston to-morrow - do you have any memorabilia of Alex's you might be able to share with me. I am putting together a memory box about him to give to the college." *Oh the lies come so easily!*

"I thought of that. I have put together some old photos. Here is one of Larry and Alex together, and a few of Alex at various times during his life. Oh, and here is their senior yearbook."

Linda had a difficult time hiding her emotions.

How could she show simple grief and nostalgia when faced with what was becoming more apparent all of the time. The pictures of young Alex did not match what she believed her husband would have looked like at that age, and a glance at the yearbook page confirmed it.

This yearbook was signed. Larry Martin had

labeled his own photo and next to it was a short message.

"Seniors rule. Stay out of trouble Alex." Larry's signature was a dead ringer for her husband Alex's distinctive handwriting, and the message from Alex - well that wasn't like his at all.

"Is Larry buried in the area," Linda asked quietly, even though she had read about it in the obituary.

"Yes, the Martins have a little plot in St. Mary's Cemetery. It is just across I-5. Take a left at the stone "Welcome To Ridgefield" marker and you'll spot it."

She wrote the directions down. She thanked Marie for her time and told her to keep in touch. "You mentioned that Larry's death was the end for your family. Do you mind if I ask you how?"

The years hadn't dimmed the sorrow. Her eyes got misty as she said, "After Larry's death, my family kind of fell apart. My mother blamed my dad for being too hard on him, on one hand, and for giving him a crazy sports car on the other. Dad blamed himself. When I turned 18, I got out of here.

"I went to Spokane to school and got married. Dad didn't last more than five years after that. Died of a heart attack. So, my husband agreed to moving here, and Mom lasted another twenty years. But things were never the same. Mom refused to leave the old house and on the surface seemed better, but I know

---

she never stopped hurting. I think it did help to have me here, but it seems like I didn't matter after Larry died. I am glad to find that Alex ended up ok after all."

Linda walked slowly back to where she had parked her car - at the town green - reflecting all the way, and sat briefly on a bench when she caught sight of a statue of a bear chasing a fish. She was charmed by the way in which the bear was positioned with his foot on a fallen tree. The fish seemed to be growing out of stones laid out like a river. All of this was not here when Alex was. Would he like the changes?

She found the graveyard easily, and after she sat and reflected at the Martin family plot, she traced the name on the headstone with her finger. Larry William Martin born April 4, 1936, died June 10, 1954. Beloved son of John and Hazel Martin. As dusk fell, she looked up to see Mt. Saint Helens to her left and Mount Hood to her right. Even the mountains are different. Before it erupted, Mt. Saint Helens had a top. Even the things we think of as most stable and unchanging are modified by the onward march of time.

As she laid the single flower she had brought upon the grave, Linda was reminded of something. *This is the second gravesite I have visited recently.*

Before she left Ridgefield, she had one more thing she needed to do. According to her map, Yale Lake was about 30 miles east from the cemetery – a

—

50-minute drive. She could see why it might take that long as she traced the winding line with her finger. "North of Chelatchie on Rt. 503," she remembered from the news article. *I guess that is the way I will go then.* It was a beautiful drive through farm fields and small towns. Eventually, the terrain became tree-lined, and as she climbed into the mountains it was easy to see how an accident might happen to the inexperienced driver. After she reached Chelatchie, her heart constricted in her chest as she drove slowly around the hairpin turns. It was only a 15-minute drive before she reached Lewis River Road but it seemed longer as she tried to imagine a young man accelerating his new sports car, going too fast, leaning into the curves. She passed a truck on her way - tall, loaded high with logs. *Maybe it was a truck like that?* She imagined a young man on the outside lane, coming up the mountain and veering slightly into the oncoming lane as he took the curve.

Then, he sees the truck and over steers back into his lane causing the car to leave the road. Alone in the car, he is trapped upon impact? Or maybe he hit his head and had died instantly?

Perhaps the truck driver did not even realize what had happened? Or maybe the driver stopped at the next town and called the police? Meanwhile, the fuel tank caught on fire and consumed both the car and the body before anyone could arrive?

As she drove back to catch her flight, her head

---

was spinning and her heart ached with an extraordinary pain. According to the photos, the man she had married was really Larry Martin. Then the corpse they found, the one they had identified as Larry, must have actually been Alex. The boys were the same height and build, and it seems that they had ID'd him simply through his belongings and other circumstantial evidence.

Somehow Alex had ended up in Larry's clothing. But a nagging thought terrified her. *Was Larry driving? Had he maybe been thrown from the car and left the scene?*

Was the man she knew as Alex directly responsible for his friend's death?

Chapter Six

Trading Places

Alex dug deep into his pockets until he found a $20 bill and handed it to young Colin Perkins who had just mowed the lawn. I know that the lawn service company pays you for this, but this is something just for you. The young boy smiled. You are the best, Professor Metzner! See you next time.

That was pretty generous, she said.

It's tough work, especially in this heat. He pushes that small gas mower over the hill out back, he whacks the weeds, and have you noticed how he pays special attention to making sure he doesn't get grass clippings in the wrong places? He actually rakes them up.

You sound like someone who knows what he is talking about. Is this something you did in your checkered past?

One job of many hard jobs that kids like me did - those with connections worked in their dad's stores, or at the worst delivered groceries. Those without connections, those without money in the family, well, we mowed lawns, dug ditches, shoveled snow, raked leaves - all hard, manual labor. But, it taught us something. It taught us discipline and the desire to work hard enough so that someday we would be paying someone else to do those things.

The trip back home had exhausted her, and Linda fell into a sleep that was dream-filled with nothing she remembered. As the sun came through the window, she became aware of where she was and what she had been through. She didn't for a moment think that all of it hadn't happened, that she had somehow dreamed it all. That is the stuff of storybooks. But the uncertainty began to fill her soul. Yes, the evidence was all there. But why?

How? Could Larry Martin have carried off being Alex Metzner for almost 60 years with no one finding out he wasn't?

No amount of coffee gave her any answers. She closed her eyes and took a deep breath, and then walked through the gap between the oaks and up to the promontory above the river. She sat down by the small gravestone and thought.

So, what now? Do I wait for you? It is all so confusing. How could I have missed it? Everything about Alex seemed so genuine. He didn't share much about his past, but when he did there was a sense of authenticity to it. Is that because, as Larry, he was so close to Alex? Did Larry mow grass or did he work in his father's office watching Alex do all of the tough jobs and then turn around and practice his free throws, and study for his exams? Could it be that in his guilt about being alive when Alex wasn't, that he finally became Alex? In his mind he believed himself to be Alex?

She stayed until the sun sank into the distance and the light breeze blew through the trees. She knew that she had to wait. There was no forcing this. But she felt she was being guided to this knowledge for a reason, and that reason just wasn't evident yet.

She went home and dialed Maureen's number. It was time to talk to someone. They met

—

for lunch the next day at Stella's Bistro. When she had gone to school in Greenbriar it was called something else, but she couldn't for the life of her remember what it was.

"The Starlight!" Maureen reminded her. "24 hours. The college students would spend hours here, cramming for exams. Now, it has gone upscale. Today's students have a little more money to spend than we did in our day, and they don't mind a little French Onion Soup Gratin washed down by a French Cabernet."

"Actually", Linda laughed, "that sounds pretty good." She handed the waitress her menu and placed her order, adding a small green salad.

The conversation started out trivially as Linda recounted the logistical problems she was having back at the house. "It turns out that I underestimated the size of my dining set. It does not fit in the dining room. And the garden - oh my - I will be hiring help I think."

"Sounds like reasons why I never moved," Maureen winked. "It is a complicated procedure."

After the chatter, they were silent for a few moments. Linda knew that Maureen was waiting. *She can tell that I have something on my mind that I need to share.*

"Hey," Linda said. "Are you done? Do you have some time to take a walk?"

"Sure. Lovely thing about being semi-retired. I only work three days a week. This is not one of them. Looks pleasant out there. Let's walk down through the park."

They settled on a bench near the fountain, and Maureen waited while they both took in a few breaths of the fresh air.

"Maureen, I have something to tell you that I am not sure you will believe. I am not sure that I believe it."

Linda didn't tell her about the spirit in the house, or about the songs, she just went straight to the punch line.

"I have reasons to believe that Alex was not who he said he was. I just got back from a trip to Ridgefield, Washington . . ."

"Oh, so that is where you were. We were looking for you down at the library."

"Yes. I went to visit a woman named Marie Martin Alcott. That is where Alex was from you know. He went to high school there. That's where he racked up the basketball and academic honors that got him into Yale."

She took a deep breath. "Maureen, I have every reason to believe that Alex was living a lie. He wasn't really Alex Metzner, but he grew up as someone named Larry Martin."

Maureen leaned back against the park bench and, twisting her body and slightly leaning back, gave Linda a long, quizzical look. "Linda. What's this about? Are you pulling my leg? I knew Alex forever. I saw his work, read his books and papers.

How could he be someone else?"

Linda didn't feel it was the right time to try to explain the singing ghost, so she just said what she had told Marie.

"I was going through Alex's things and realized that he had not kept anything from his high school days. I thought it would be great to get a yearbook and make a memorial. I am collecting other memorabilia too. So, I found a Facebook page from his high school and an old classmate responded to my query and sent me a yearbook. Marie, the picture that looked most like my Alex was named Larry Martin. Just below it was a picture that didn't look like him labeled Alex Metzner."

"Well, it may have been a mistake," she said. "Or people change. I know I don't look anything like my senior portrait."

"Yes, I thought about that as well. But it kept nagging at me. Why did Alex have so little from those days? He kept everything from Yale. So, that is why I figured I needed to go to Ridgefield. I took it on face value that the reason he didn't want to ever go back there was because he had been an orphan and had no family. But, Maureen, he had been such a good student and an outstanding athlete. It seemed strange that he did not want to go back to see old high school chums."

"So, what did you find out in Ridgefield? Did this woman know anything? Who was she anyway?"

"Before I left, I found obituaries. This boy, Larry Martin, had been killed in a car crash right after graduation. They mentioned a sister, Marie, and I was able to track her down. It turns out that he was a friend of Alex and that Alex was supposed to be in the car that night but wasn't. After the accident, Alex wrote a letter claiming he felt he had let Larry down by not driving back with him - that Larry would not have died if he had gone with him. Out of guilt, he just wanted to move on with his life. Alex never returned to Ridgefield.

"I told Marie what I've told you - that I was wanting some high school memorabilia of Alex's and she was nice enough to find Larry's old yearbook. Maureen, there were those faces again. I pointed at Larry and said, is this your brother? She said yes it was. But this time there were signatures. You know what distinctive handwriting Alex had? Well, there was a little note from Alex to Larry that didn't look like Alex's handwriting at all, but the note from Larry to Alex - well, it was a dead ringer for my husband's handwriting."

"Oh my. It does sound strange, but still circumstantial, don't you think. And how could he have pulled it off, and why? I mean he'd need ID, right? And transcripts to take Alex's place at Yale."

"Yes, I know. I have been thinking about that. Larry was totally disfigured in the car crash Maureen. They identified him by items he had on

---

him. He was perfectly unrecognizable. And, I am sure that so many years ago things were much more relaxed than they are now. With Alex's birth certificate Larry would have been able to get a new ID in New Haven, and then the transcripts and everything would have fallen into place."

Maureen looked at Linda and asked, "There is something else isn't there?"

Linda sighed, looked down, and said quietly, "Yes. But I am not ready to talk about that. Soon. I will tell you soon." Linda walked slowly back to the house and just sat there in the dusk until it turned to dark and then into moon and stars. The crickets began their song and still she sat. Finally, she went into the kitchen and poured herself a glass of wine, lit a fire, and sat some more. She thought about putting on some music, but there was only one kind of music she wanted to hear. Will she come back again? Will she let me know? The warmth of the fire and wine soon had her drowsy. Her head lay against the back of the brown velour couch, and half asleep and half awake she wasn't sure if it was a dream or not. The music came and through half-opened eyes Linda saw her. She was a little more defined this time.

She began to see the shape of her face. *Perhaps she is starting to trust me.* She reached for her phone and pressed 'record' – this time she wasn't going to trust her memory.

In the morning, she listened to the song in

---

the light of day. There it was. She hadn't dreamed it.

Silver Coins

A silver coin has two sides
And if you were to choose
And you could rig the game of life
Would it be heads you win, tails you lose?
A rich boy thought that he would like
To be a poor man for a day.
The poor boy thought, yeah, what the hell
See how the rich boys play.
A sweatshirt for a jacket,
A T-shirt for a tie.
A prince and a pauper
Headed out one night.
A silver coin has two sides
And if you were to choose
And you could rig the game of life
Would it be heads you win, tails you lose?
The rich boy had an easy life,
He'd always had a home,
Never had to earn his keep
In a cold world all alone.
The poor boy lived from house to house
He'd always had to pay
With hard work and perseverance
To get by from day to day.
A silver coin has two sides

And if you were to choose
And you could rig the game of life
Would it be heads you win, tails you lose?
The rich boy told the poor boy,
We will switch IDs.
Tonight I will be you.
Tonight you can be me.
They headed out together
But ended up alone.
One fled to find his fortune
The other is beneath a stone.
A silver coin has two sides
And if you were to choose
And you could rig the game of life
Would it be heads you win, tails you lose?
Don't jump to conclusions,
Falls are caused by pride.
Remember that a silver coin
Always has two sides.

Once again she thanked God for hot showers. Really. Is there anything more blissful that we take for granted? She spent longer than she should have under the cascade from the modern rain shower-head that had been installed in the updated bath.

After hearing the song the night before, she had felt as if she couldn't comprehend it all. She had fallen into a restless sleep with the chorus repeating over and over. However, in the midst of it all another song kept trying to interrupt. It was as if the young singer was trying to say, "Ok you know about Alex, now I want you to know about me." *I guess I will hear it soon enough.*

In the meantime, she finally had to admit that Alex was Larry. He had pulled of some kind of great con and lived a life of deception. The song cemented it. They had deliberately changed places, each deciding to be a different person just to see how it felt. But, did Larry kill Alex? Was Larry at the wheel? Had he been thrown from the car? Maybe then he just took advantage of the situation. The boy who never was good enough could now achieve something for a change.

Linda wondered if Alex - or Larry as it seems to be - ever wanted to go back and tell his father, see Dad, see? I could do it. I am a success. I went to Yale. I became a professor. Are you proud of me now?

But could he have gone back? His dad died just five years after he left - before he had even finished his PhD. Even so, the triumph of success would have been overshadowed by his deception. And maybe - and the thought chilled her - her husband did have something to do with Alex's death? She decided it was time to fully confide in Maureen. *I have the recorded song. Proof, right? That I am not crazy?*

She wanted to make Maureen a nice dinner and share a glass of wine by the fire. It would make it easier to open up to her.

—

"Linda, this Chicken Marengo is fantastic. I haven't had such a good meal in a long time. I hope that Alex appreciated this!"

"Well, I didn't cook like this when I was still working," she laughed. "But yes, when I did get a chance to cook, Alex was very appreciative."

They sat together and stared into the fire.

"So," Maureen said, "I think you have something to tell me?"

"Yes," she answered, "I have to tell someone."

And so, Linda related to Maureen all that had happened and played her the song she had captured on her phone.

Maureen sat there in dazed silence for a moment. "Well," she said. "That is really something. Do you think? Is this true, Linda? Are you haunted?"

"I think so Maureen. I have trouble believing it too. But this girl is trying to tell me something. I am meant to know much more than that Alex wasn't Alex. That is just the prelude. There is more to these songs than I know so far."

Linda took a sip of her wine and said, "There is another song coming. I keep hearing bits of it. Somehow, I think I need to go back to the stone. Will you come with me?"

"Maybe the spirit won't come back if you share this?"

"I don't know. But I do know I can't do it alone.

I have been down to the gravestone on my own before, but that was . . . before. Plus, I need to share this with someone. Maybe you will see something out there that I don't."

"Ok. Would Saturday morning be ok? The weather is supposed to be good. How about I drop by after breakfast? 10?"

"I think that will be perfect. Maybe something else will come before that, but if it doesn't, we will go in search of it."

The next two nights were blissfully calm and Linda received no visitations. *Is she waiting for me I wondered? Does she know I am coming to the grave? It is there in the walls, this plaintive, distant sound. It is like a musical breeze. It touches my skin and hair but I can't pin down. It is coming. I will find out soon.*

Saturday was clear, as Maureen had predicted, and she arrived promptly at 10, dressed in hiking pants, boots, and sun hat.

Linda laughed. "The walk isn't terribly tough, but wow, you look great. I love it!"

Maureen smiled back impishly. "Well it isn't often I get invited to trek through the underbrush in search of ghosts. I did want to be prepared."

"Oh, Maureen. I love you. I really needed this. Just give me a moment and I will be with you."

She jumped into Levis and a T-shirt, and because Maureen was right about the hat in the bright sunshine, she grabbed a visor as well.

—

They took a long look at each other, took in a couple of breaths, and shut the door behind them.

Linda had been back to the place by the river since that first day when she found the gravestone, so she was able to warn Maureen about the undergrowth, and she went first to brush away the tree limbs.

"Ha!" Maureen said. "I guess I was right about wearing my outdoor gear. These pants are snag resistant and my boots wouldn't know how to slip if you asked them to."

Ah Maureen. Always good for a laugh. She chuckled. "Yep, you got me again. I will probably be picking pine needles out of my T-shirt for days."

It was actually a lovely walk. Since the land belonged to the house, and was private property, no one went down there. Alex used to clear the path when they were first married, but it was obvious no one had taken over that duty.

When they got to the bottom of the ravine, the water was low and they were able to hop across it, stone by stone. After that, it was a short climb to the promontory.

It was still there - the gravestone. It was smaller than she remembered, and the area was overgrown. She was not sure anyone casually hiking in the area would have even noticed it.

Maureen stopped suddenly when Linda drew back the high grass and revealed it. She removed her hat and knelt down.

"Oh my" she whispered. "Linda, what is this? It really is quite lovely. However, I don't think it is professionally done. Or, maybe just done in haste? The engraving is a bit rustic looking.

"You had no idea it was here? But wait, you haven't been here for forty years. Have you researched the previous owners and been able to ask anyone about it?" She furrowed her brow, thinking deeply.

"No. I need to do that. I guess I was so overwhelmed by the feeling I got about it. When the ghost appeared, I just felt there was a connection. Maybe now, once I get over the shock about Alex, I can start thinking about this grave and the connection it has to the house and to my singing ghost."

She then said quietly, "This is where Alex proposed to me. We moved in after our May wedding and left in the autumn of that same year. 1972."

"I didn't realize you guys had not been here very long. I guess someone could have brought remains, maybe ashes? After you guys left? Someone who had a reason to want to put the ashes here, in this spot?"

"Well, that seems like one likely possibility. But I don't get a feeling of happiness here Maureen. There is a weight of immense sadness on my shoulders as I stand here. I can't shake it."

"Do you think it is the girl in the house is

---

who is buried there? It would seem to make sense. But why isn't she haunting the grave? Why the house? Perhaps if you came out here in the evening, alone, she would appear here?"

"I don't think I could do that Maureen. I will have to wait to see if she tells me more. I have a feeling she haunts the house for a reason."

Maureen looked me in the eye. "Maybe her death happened there? And maybe now, after all these years, you are the catalyst. In you she has found an open, responsive soul who will listen."

Linda's breath was shaky as she exhaled. "Yes, I think you are right. She wants me to know something - she wants me to do something. I guess I will find out. But there is also the possibility that she is just a spirit who haunts the house and wants to relay its secrets. They may have something to do with her or not."

"You don't feel afraid of personal harm to you Linda? Like this girl might turn into poltergeist and overturn your bed when you are sleeping or something like that?"

"No. I don't feel as if I am in any danger. Any physical danger anyway." She laughed nervously. "My emotions are taking a hit though."

Maureen took her elbow. "Let's get back. I think you have had enough for today."

They walked back in silence.

"Do you want me to stay the night?" she asked kindly.

"No. But thank you. I need to be alone. I don't think the spirit will come if someone is with me. And I need to prepare myself. It is all about listening isn't it Maureen? That is something we have a hard time doing in our fast-paced society. I must be alone and I must listen. She told me about Alex. Now there must be something else she has to say - about this stone."

Chapter Seven

Dear Diary

"I love the flower girl, was she reality or just a dream to me." Linda remembers the days when she was a big fan of the Cowsills. This had been a favorite song. She decided from then on that the ghost girl would be the flower girl, and she eagerly awaited her next visit.

It didn't take long. It was as if that trip to the grave opened a door, and that night Linda was awakened by a song. The tune was familiar. It was a tune that had been blowing around her through the last few days, but now she heard it distinctly.

Linda sat up in bed and there she was. Each time she came, she was a little more fleshed out. Tonight she could see that she was very young. The shape of her mouth came into focus and she sang with her eyes closed.

She was no longer scared. The spirit was obviously asking for help. She had left her phone on her nightstand and it was on and ready to record. Her mind had held things in the past, but she didn't want to rely on that. Every word of these songs was important. She was sure of that now.

After the last note faded, so did the flower girl. Linda sat still for a while, but then she knew she needed to sleep. She told her mind to let it go and to listen to it in the light. *Think of this academically. This is research.*

Interestingly enough, she did sleep well. When she woke up this time, she didn't ask if it was a dream. She knew it wasn't. She got her coffee, took a shower, and then sat in the kitchen and started her phone.

It was there. This time it was delicate. She had a lovely voice. It reminded her of Joan Baez or Joni Mitchell. Didn't they all want to be Joni back then?

Dear Diary the place where I confide
Dear Diary, the things I hold inside.
I need a place to hide my diary.
She leans into the corner

———

Upon a hardwood floor
And she asks her diary
What her love is for.
Life is like a crossword puzzle
Filled with love and loss.
The answer's sometimes 6 squares down
And also 3 across . . .
Dear Diary the place where I confide
Dear Diary, the things I hold inside.
I need a place to hide my diary.
The light is getting dim
From 48 panes of glass
So she writes by the light of the moon
As it shines upon the grass.
She can't use the light
Of that crystal chandelier,
Somebody might see
somebody might hear.
Dear Diary the place where I confide
Dear Diary, the things I hold inside.
I need a place to hide my diary.

Diaries. We all kept those, back in the day. We didn't have computers and phones. There was no social media to spill our guts to. We wrote, by hand, in diaries.

Linda remembered her diary. It was about 5 x 7, blue with gold flowers and simply inscribed, "My Diary". She smiled to herself.

You would think that it would be evident.

—

But, no, diaries had one purpose and woe be to those who used these books in any other capacity!

During the last few years, in her classes, she had had many discussions with her students about this. They insisted that privacy wasn't a big deal to them. People usually wanted to vent their problems to the whole world.

Well, this might be possible now, but when she was young, diaries were sacred places of the spirit and heart. Could it be that this young girl had left a diary somewhere? In the house? *Is that what I am meant to find?*

However, if she expected some kind of quick resolution to the story she would be expecting too much. She heard nothing from the spirit in the next few days, so she kept busy doing what it is she was trained to do: research.

But before she headed down to the county courthouse, it seemed that the best place to start would be with someone who already knew a lot about the owners of this house, so she put in a call to her realtor.

"Hello, Cassie. This is Linda Metzner."

"Linda! I hope you are settling in well. Nothing's wrong I hope?"

"Oh no. No, I just had a few minor questions about the house and was hoping to talk with the previous owners. Do you have records for them?"

"Well, the Turners are the ones you bought

it from. You met them. They had the place for over 20 years. Raised their whole family there. I am not sure who had the house before that. Before my time. But you know, rather than make you go down to the Courthouse to the registry, I can find out for you quickly."

"I can help a little." Linda said. "I still have copies of the original bill of sale, and we sold the house to someone called William and Constance Burnette. But that is all I know."

"Ok. I will start there. Get back to you soon. I have some clients coming, but once I am free it shouldn't take long."

In less than an hour she called back. "Hi Linda. Looks like the house sold in 1972, as you say, to William and Constance Burnette. They moved here from Kansas City, Missouri. They only stayed in the house for two years while William taught at Greenbriar High. I don't know where they went from here. It lay empty for a long time until it sold to a John Abbott in 1981. Then, a couple named Joseph and Elise Ferrell were in it until the Turners bought it. That is about all I can do for you. That's what you could find out for yourself at the registry. If you are looking to contact the previous owners, well, that would be up to you. It is out of the scope of my ethical responsibility."

"Oh, of course Cassie. I understand. I can take it from here. Thanks so much."

After a few days at the county clerk's office,

she had tracked down all of the previous owners. According to the bank records, they had moved back to Kansas City, Missouri where they were from. There were no white pages results for them. An obituary search in the Kansas City Star did yield results. They were both dead, and they had had no children. It ended there.

But the search for John Abbot was more fruitful. After searching through many John Abbots, it seemed that the one who had occupied her house was an academic and was currently a professor emeritus at the University of Toronto.

First, she contacted the Turners. They were a young couple just starting out when they bought the house, and she was able to track them down. She knew their ages, full names, and approximate birthdates. She also knew that they were originally from Brunswick, Maine, so when a general Internet search found a couple that matched this inform- ation, she felt comfortable enough to call.

"Hello. I am looking for Wayne or Janet Turner."

"This is Wayne speaking. What can I do for you?" His voice had that quizzical pitch that indicated he supposed that she was trying to sell him something.

"This is Linda Metzner. You bought my house in Greenbriar, Vermont, twenty years ago."

"Oh yes, Linda! I remember meeting you at the closing. I hear that you purchased the house back.

"I am sorry we weren't there, but we had left the property several months before. Sorry about your husband. I heard from Ms. Milquist that he passed away."

"Thank you. Yes, he did. I decided I wanted to come back to Greenbriar where we had been so happy."

"What can I do for you," he asked.

"Well, this may seem odd, but I have a question about the back property. I am considering sub-dividing and ran into a little snag. The surveyors found what seems to be a cemetery down near the river. We want to find out who might be buried there and get permission before going any further. There is only one stone and it is a simple one, but it wasn't present when Alex and I lived there. I was wondering if you knew anything about it."

"That's funny. I also wondered the same thing. I used to go down to the river with the kids, it was my favorite place to walk, and I stumbled upon it. I thought maybe it was just someone's idea of a joke. Since it was small and fairly homemade looking, I just let it be. Up there on the promontory it really wasn't in the way. I guess after that, I forgot about it. Interesting isn't it. So someone thinks it might be real, eh?"

"Well, we need to examine every possibility before we begin destroying hallowed ground," she

---

laughed. "I appreciate your time."

"No problem. Hey, enjoy being back home."

"I will," she said. "Take care."

So, the stone was there when the Turners bought the house in 1996. *I know who I have to call next.*

"Good morning Linda! So nice to hear from you," Georgia Bemis said cordially. "Is this a social call, or is there something I can do for you."

"Well, I am a little embarrassed to say it is the latter. I do hope that you and I will have time to chat soon, but I am still in the throes of settling in. I was hoping that you, the fountain of all information ala Greenbriar, might be able to help me. I need to get some information about renovations that might have been done to the house and am trying to track down the man who owned it between 1981 and 1985 - a fellow named John Abbot. I believe he is an academic and wondered if he might have taught at Greenbriar."

"Well, that is fairly easy because John Abbot did teach here and was a visiting professor in Anthropology. He was quite well known on campus and did, indeed, live in your house. I believe when he left here that he was hired by the University of Toronto. Sorry to say, I don't know what became of him after that."

"Mrs. Bemis, you are an angel. Yes, I tracked a John Abbott to Toronto and just wanted to make sure I had the right one before I went any further. The other people I am trying to track down are Joseph and Elise Ferrell. I haven't had a chance to do any research on them, so thought I would check with you first."

"Oh yes. Joe is still in town. He and Elise divorced, and she moved back to Omaha with the two kids. Joe still has his law practice. You know it. Ferrell and Langston, down on Third Street."

"Yes, that sounds very familiar. You are a godsend. You just saved me a whole lot of trouble."

"Oh no trouble! Looking forward to having a nice long visit once you get settled in. Good luck!"

As Linda approached Third Street, she remembered the place. Like many other offices in an historic New England town, Ferrell and Langston had their headquarters in an old, white Cape Cod style house fringed by oaks and framed with a perfect green lawn. Their business sign was tasteful and discreet enough to satisfy the town fathers who liked their businesses to be seen but not broadcast. A tasteful, old established company.

She walked into the house and was greeted by a trim woman who sat behind a desk that had been positioned in front of the old fireplace.

"Good morning," she said cheerfully. "May I help you?"

"Yes, I was hoping to talk with Joe Ferrell. My name is Linda Harner Metzner. "

"Old Joe or young Joe?" she queried.

———

"Well, I am looking for the Joe Ferrell who once lived in a house at 71 Minot Street. He was married to Elise Ferrell. I currently live in that house, and I have a question for him."

"Ah yes, that would be Joe Sr. He is semi-retired and isn't in the office today, but let me see if Joe Jr. is available. He lived there as child and might be able to help you. He can certainly connect you with his dad."

"Sure. That would be great." Joe Jr., a handsome man of about 40, greeted her with a smile and a handshake. "Mrs. Metzner! Delighted to meet you. I saw in the Greenbriar news that your husband had passed and that you had resettled in town. First of all, my condolences on his passing. What can I do for you? I hear that you have a question about the old house? I have very fond memories of that house. I am glad you were able to repurchase it, for memory's sake. Is there a problem?"

"Not a problem, really." She went on to spin the same tale she had given Wayne Turner. "I was hoping your dad might have some insight into the stone. You lived there from 1985-1996 I believe."

"Yes we did." He paused and tilted his head reflectively. "I used to walk down in that area all of the time. I loved it! You are referring to the small outcropping above the river?"

"Yes, that is the one."

"I do remember a very small stone marker

there. But I didn't think too much of it. It had a small flower on it?

"That's the one. I would like to know whether it is part of a larger cemetery perhaps, an old one? Or if it is a one-off burial, maybe I could dig it up and have it put into the town cemetery?"

"You know, I stopped going down there when I was about 15. I was too involved in sports and school. But my sister and I used to build little forts on that promontory. We pretended that we were defending it against the Indians. We called the stone Clementine's Grave. But then Mom and Dad split up, and she took my brother and sister with her and went back to Omaha, I stopped going out there then and pretty much forgot about it."

"Thanks Mr. Ferrell. I take it you didn't go back to Nebraska with your mother?

"No, I was in high school by then and didn't want to leave. I stayed to attend Greenbriar and then after law school went into practice with Dad. If you still want to talk with him, he comes into the office on Wednesdays and Fridays."

She thanked him and smiled. "I am sure that your memory will suffice. But say hello to your dad for me, and if either of you wants to come for a visit, please just give me a call."

"Sure enough." And he laughed, "If you want any legal advice on that stone, let me know."

"Thanks" she said, just a jovially. "I will."

Two down, one to go. She knew someone on

the faculty in the University of Toronto. The woman had been a student of hers, so Linda gave her a call that afternoon. Lisa was in her office, thank goodness. She didn't think she could drag this out much longer.

"Dr. Metzner! It is so nice to hear from you. I was just thinking of you the other day when the Literature Committee was deciding whether or not to take *Middlemarch* off the required reading list. I didn't think you would approve."

"Certainly not. What did they want to replace it with? Something more current that the students will 'relate' to?"

"Yeah, several authors that you would not approve of were mentioned. But I doubt this is a social call - I sense you have a question for me."

"I do, in fact. Do you know a John Abbott there - I believe he is still a professor emeritus in the Anthropology department."

"Yes, he is. He teaches one graduate course. Thursdays I think. Do you need to speak to him before then? He doesn't often come into his office. I have his home number if you'd like."

"Yes, I'd like that very much - thank you Lisa. But before I do that, please fill me in on what is going on with you if you have a minute."

After their little chat, Linda dialed the number she had given her.

"Hello, is this John Abbott?"

"Speaking."

"My name is Linda Harner Metzner. I used to live in the same house that you occupied in Greenbriar, Vermont, when you taught at the college."

"Oh, yes! How are you? Yours and Dr. Metzner's reputations preceded you. I was sorry to not have met you. What can I do for you?"

Once more, she repeated her fabrication.

"That is certainly very interesting," he said. "But I am sorry to say, I can't help you very much. I walked out to the river once during the entire time I was there, and I didn't climb up any ridge. If there was a stone there, I was unlikely to have seen it."

After a few more pleasantries, she hung up. Well, she had narrowed things by a little bit. She knew that the stone was placed there sometime after she and Alex left in 1972 and before the Ferrells moved there in1985. 15 years is a lot of territory to cover.

The flower girl had led her to Alex's true identity and also down to the stone by the river. But Linda still didn't know if the two things were connected or not, and so she had to keep researching the stone.

But how does it all relate to the flower girl? Would she be leading me to this stuff if it didn't apply to her? Something in all of this must have led to her death.

She couldn't help but think Emily Bronte, steeped as she was in 19th century English Lit.

Is the ghost I see and hear real, or just symbolism and allegory? Is the flowergirl a kind of time-warped Catherine and is her Heathcliff yet to come? Does he roam the grassy promontory as well?

Perhaps just my imagination as I struggle with my own grief?

"I lingered round them, under that benign sky; watched the moths fluttering among the heath, and harebells; listened to the soft wind breathing through the grass; and wondered how anyone could ever imagine unquiet slumbers for the sleepers in that quiet earth."

Emily Bronte, <u>Wuthering Heights</u>

Chapter Eight

The Burnettes

The next morning, Linda looked over the lyrics to the songs. *There is a connection somewhere, and I have to find that diary.*

She met Maureen for lunch.

"So," Maureen said eagerly. "How did it go? Did you find anything out from Joe Ferrell?"

Linda related what had happened at the meeting. "So, it seems that the stone was put there sometime between 1972 and 1985, but I am not any closer than that."

She told Maureen about her Emily Bronte fantasy. At first she laughed at Linda's dramatic imagination, but then she suddenly turned serious. "Well, you might not be too far wrong. There must be much sadness in your ghost's past. Any luck on the diary?"

"No," she sighed. "I think the key to finding it is in the lyrics to the songs. Meanwhile, as I try to put two and two together, I think I will find out anything I can on the Burnettes."

Her first stop on the way home was to the County Clerk's office. Linda explained her situation. The clerk said she would look into locating the mortgage records for the Burnettes and give Linda a call when she found them.

Meanwhile, Linda went back to her computer where she had saved the obituaries she had found.

William Francis Burnette, 72, Kansas City and formerly of Greenbriar, VT. Beloved teacher, father, and husband passed away peacefully in his home after a long illness on January 27th, 2001. He is survived by Constance, his wife of 43 years. Burnette taught history at Park Hill High School for 20 years and graduated from Missouri State University with a Masters in Education in 1952. He was hired by Central High School in Springfield, Missouri. He left Springfield to teach at Greenbriar High in Greenbriar, Vermont for two years before returning to Missouri. Visitation will be 3-8 p.m.

Thursday, January 31, at Passantino Bros. Funeral Home, 2117 Independence Blvd., Kansas City, MO, 64124. Family and friends will gather on Friday, March 23, at Mount Olivet Mausoleum, 7601 Blue Ridge Blvd., Raytown, MO 64138, where the Rosary will be prayed at 10:30 a.m. followed by entombment.

Constance Jean (Simmons) Burnette, 80, of Kansas City and formerly Greenbriar, Vermont, passed away at Elmhurst Nursing Home on May 6, 2009. She was preceded in death by her husband, William Francis Burnette. A lifelong homemaker, Constance was an active member of the Friends of the Library at the Kansas City Library, and a communicant of the Cathedral of the Immaculate Conception. A funeral mass will be held at her church, 416 W 12th Street, Kansas City, on Tuesday, May 10th at 4 p.m., followed by burial next to her husband of 43 years in the Mount Olivet Mausoleum, 7601 Blue Ridge Blvd. Raytown, MO 64138.

No extended family was mentioned. No children. Linda began to think that if there were anything to be found out about the Burnettes that was of importance, it would be in Greenbriar.

She decided to go talk to some folks down at the high school the next day to see what she could find out.

Meanwhile, she was very tired. She made

—

herself a cup of cocoa and tried to stay up to think things through, but it was of no use. She tucked herself into bed and slipped into a fitful sleep. She thought she dreamed that she came - the flower girl - but she had no voice. *Perhaps she has said all she will to me. Maybe she is waiting for me to digest what she has already given me. I am trying, I told her. I am trying.*

In the light of the morning she felt rested, if not entirely refreshed. She took her coffee out to the sunroom and pulled out the lyrics she had. *The answer has to be in the Dear Diary song.*

Linda studied the lyrics. It seems that the flower girl was trying to tell her where she hid the diary. *It has to be in this house. After all, this is where she is haunting.*

Hardwood floors. Well, that didn't help much. The entire house had hardwood floors. But, she realized, only one room had 48 panes of glass and an old crystal chandelier. Although a lot of upgrades had been made, not much had been done to the large bedroom adjacent to the master. Four double-hung windows, with 12 panes each, still lined one entire wall of the room. *That equals 48.*

Perhaps it had seemed too overwhelming to replace all of those windows with energy-efficient replacements. Instead, they had just been covered with plastic.

The room also had an enormous crystal light fixture so immense, historic, and expensive, that it still lit the big room and had also never been replaced.

She walked up the stairs to see if she remembered correctly. *Yes, that is right. 48 panes of glass and a crystal chandelier. Hardwood floor.*

"She leans into a corner" . . . well, there were four corners. However, only one corner had light from a window overlooking the lawn. "She writes by the light of the moon as it shines upon the grass."

Ok, now what? So, she wrote in her diary in this room. Linda sat in the corner and pulled out the lyrics again. Crossword puzzle? There was nothing at all in the house when she had moved in, certainly no random pieces of paper. But the singer didn't say it was a real puzzle. She sang that life is "like" a crossword puzzle. Linda shut her eyes and took a deep breath. Then she opened them again and suddenly she saw it.

The wall she leaned up against was lined with windows. The wall just to her right, perpendicular to the window wall was paneled. Again, nothing had been done to this room in the way of modernization, and the panel took up the entire wall. The panel was made up of a series of trimmed squares. They went from floor to ceiling, interrupted only by a radiator near the middle, and one clerestory window near the ceiling.

As she sat in her corner by the window, she counted: three squares across. Then, looking up at the ceiling she counted down 6 squares. She realized that the paneled wall protruded about six inches from the window above. The wall had been added later, she thought. Perhaps furring strips were required in order to tack it up over the original plaster.

She ran down to the shed in the yard, hoping that the tools had been left behind, and found a two-prong hammer and a screwdriver. Using the flat-head screwdriver as a pry tool, she was able to remove the top of the trim that framed the panel. With the prongs of the hammer, she pried off the rest.

Beneath the trim there were a series of screws holding the panel, and she was able to quickly remove them. She pulled gently on the square piece of wood and it yielded easily. There, wrapped in paper was a small book-sized object. She reached in and unwrapped it. On the cover were the words, "My Diary", and below them was a flower. It was a flower just like the one on the gravestone. There was also a key in a velvet envelope. She looked at it and saw the numbers "111". She could not see that it had any connection to the diary, which did not need a key, so she put the key in her jewelry box and gave her attention to the diary.

"Are you sure Linda?" Maureen asked later. "That might mean that it is your ghost is who is buried out there."

"Yes, that has occurred to me."

"So, have you read the diary? What kinds of things are in it? Do you know a name?"

She sighed. "I just looked through it briefly. I haven't had the fortitude to look closely. Maybe I am afraid of what I will find. Maybe I just want it to say 'April Fools! Nothing to see here.'" She laughed a little ruefully.

"I can understand that," Maureen said. "But given what you already know, I think that maybe reading the diary can help you finish this all up."

"Yeah, you are right. I am going to hole up for a while and put the investigation about the Burnettes on hold."

That evening, Linda took the book to her favorite chair overlooking the garden. She made sure that there would be enough light as the sun went down.

Dear Diary:

Well, dear diary, I bought you so that I could chronicle my thoughts about this new life.

Missoula is so far away. I still can't believe that I had the nerve to come here - all the way to Vermont. My first impression? It is so leafy here! Will I miss the open sky and learn to love the green mountains?

My classes are good so far, but I am a little disappointed about what seems to be a lack of political activism on campus. Just a bunch of kids throwing Frisbees and talking about the ski season.

No one seems to care about the war and there is a really big ROTC program here. Maybe I should have gone to Berkeley. Oh how my heart yearns for something bigger. My classes are fine, and I am doing well academically. In fact, I have been kept too busy to write in this diary! I go from my dorm to the cafeteria, to class, to the library and back again. I never have been one for sports but I have even gone to the football games. Should I stay? I mean, here I am ensconced in a place just as conservative as the one I came from. Maybe I will look to transfer in a year. However, I do like this guy - MT - he's pretty fabulous. Might keep me here.

Linda paused to absorb some of this and to jot down some notes. She now had some things to go on while trying to find out the identity of the flower girl. She had a time period and a place of origin.

There was much in the diary that she wasn't quite sure she understood, but this MT character was someone else she could research. Sounds like he may have been somebody.

Chapter Nine

Gladys

Flickering light and shadow danced on the wall through the gap in the blackout curtains. A glance at the clock told Linda that she had slept soundly through the night until 8:30.

Wow! No dreams, no music? Maybe the diary will be the last of it. She knew that she would have to go back and read it more carefully, but right now she knew she had to focus on the Burnettes.

Maybe that is what the flower girl wanted her to find out. This thought seemed to clear and clarify her mind, and she began to plan how to find out more about the short stay in Greenbriar of William and Constance Burnette.

"Hmm . . . I wonder", she murmured. When in doubt, ask the secretary. She remembered Gladys Evans as a cheerful blonde who greeted everyone who walked the halls of Greenbriar High School. It seemed very likely that she would remember William Burnette. She had been married here and her husband been a local businessman. There was a good chance they had stayed in town.

She sipped her coffee quietly and searched through whitepages.com. Gladys Evans. 71 Union Street. Yay! A phone number too. *Glad I am not the only one who still keeps a landline.*

Her fingered paused as they touched the keypad on her cordless phone. One landline to another; it somehow seemed in keeping with the time-spanning events.

"Hello?"

"Is this Gladys Thomas, formerly Gladys Evans?"

"Well, yes. Evans is my maiden name."

"Great! This is Linda Harner Metzner. You and I go way back. I was an adjunct professor at Greenbriar in the early 70's."

"Well, I am sure I would remember if I saw you! I met so many people."

"I am sure you did! But I don't expect you to remember me. I am hoping that you remember someone who used to teach there. William Burnette?"

A pause. "Oh yes, I remember William. He was here for only two years. From down South somewhere."

"Yes," Linda said. "That's right. Kansas City, Missouri."

"Of course. What is it you want to know?"

"Can I come visit, Mrs. Evans? I have just moved back into the area, and it would be great to touch base with folks who lived here back then as well."

"Well, sure. I guess that would be ok. Are you free this afternoon?"

Union Street wasn't very far away, and Linda knocked on the door promptly at two. A familiar, if older, face greeted her at the door with a big smile, "Yes! I do remember you. Senior Experience? You came and gave a talk to the students about Greenbriar College!

Linda laughed. "Good memory!"

"Come on in! I have some tea for us."

Linda settled back in a comfy chair and, for awhile, she and Gladys chatted about where their lives had taken them. It turns out that Gladys was a widow as well. She had stayed in Greenbriar after her retirement.

"My two kids are still nearby, so it made sense for me to stay."

"Yes, perfect sense. You stayed at the school the whole time? And with all the people who have come and gone you remember Mr. Burnette?"

Gladys lowered her eyes in an uncomfortable way. "A situation like Bill Burnette's doesn't come along often. Is he still alive?"

Linda told her what she had found out about the Burnettes.

"Well, I guess even though I was taught to not talk ill of the dead, it wouldn't hurt to just tell what I know. Why is it you are interested? You weren't here when the Burnettes were."

"No, but they bought our house after we left."

"Oh, yes. That's right. The lovely old house on Minot Street. Professor Metzner and you lived there for awhile after your marriage."

"That's right. There are some things about the house that are unsettled, and I wondered if you could give me any insight into the Burnettes when they lived there."

"Well, Bill Burnette was a friend of Principal Harris. I guess they had gone to school together. When an unexpected opening occurred in the History Department, Principal Harris encouraged him to move here.

"They were amiable people and it seemed that they were going to fit in quite fine. But little by little, with first gossip and then confirmation, it became evident that Bill Burnette had a tough time keeping his hands off the girl students."

Oh really? Something about this is making

sense to me. "Did he ever mention having a young woman stay at his house?"

She thought hard. "Yes, I do believe that they brought in a girl for the summer as a housemaid to Mrs. Burnette, who had some heath issues. I don't know her name. I don't think she stayed long. In fact, I seem to remember some gossip surrounding that as well. She left town suddenly."

"Was this . . . tendency . . . of Bill Burnette's the reason he didn't stay in Greenbriar?"

"I think maybe it was. I know I remember there were many parents in and out of the Principal's office, and a sudden decision by the Burnettes to go back to Georgia that necessitated a quick search for a replacement. The common thought was Mrs. Burnette's health - at least on the surface."

Gladys paused and asked skeptically, "So exactly what do all these questions have to do with the house?"

"Oh, there were a few things left behind that I was hoping to get to their rightful owners, and some repair work that I didn't understand. But, it looks like I will have to accept that I am too late. If anything else comes to mind about the girl who might have stayed there, please give me a call. I have found something that she might want after all these years. A diary. It is not filled with many specifics unfortunately, and there is no name on it.

"However, I still think I would like to be able

to return it to her. Thanks for your help."

"Well, certainly. I am glad all of my years at Greenbriar High could be of some value."

Chapter Ten

Michael

Dear Diary
I am so shaken. Today a building on campus went up in flames. There was smoke everywhere and I just stood on the sidewalk not knowing what to do. The firefighters were gathered around but they were frozen too. No one did anything. Before I could think, I felt a firm hand grab my waist and a voice whispered. "Come with me. You'll be safe here." I felt myself being propelled into an empty classroom and when I turned my eyes met his. Piercing and bright with an intelligence and fervor

unlike any eyes I have ever seen. It's ok he said, my name is Michael. You can trust me. I whispered my name back to him. What is going on? I asked.

Revolt against the murders at Kent State. Someone has decided to burn the Consecration Hall in protest. But why aren't the firefighters doing anything I asked. I think they are worried that they will be shot. He laughed dryly. And they might be. Authority. Authority in this country has gone crazy. If we don't respect the right to protest in this country, this is what happens. Anarchy. Hey, you want to come to a meeting? Just a little something I organize. It's all wrong. If we don't stop it, who will? We talked well into the night. Michael is amazing. This is what I was searching for when I left Montana.

It was late morning. The shutters were still closed and Linda sat with her coffee cup and stared at the light coming through the slats. "I need to get up. Get going. There is much to do, much to do . . ."

But was there, she wondered? So, Gladys had given her some things to chew on. Bill Burnette was known for his "tendency" to violate young girls. But she hadn't found any connection between the flower girl and Bill Burnette.

Linda slowly got up and put her coffee cup in the sink, then went to the kitchen window and opened the shutters. The morning was calm and sunny and she said aloud, "I have to let this go.

There is nothing more that I can do." *But there is. I might not be able to find out what happened to her, but I can find out who she is. Maybe that is all she wants.*

She ran a comb through her long hair and stared at herself in the mirror. She had pretty much decided long ago to not pay attention to the signs of age. Her eyes were still so young. Alex had loved her eyes. He had once told her, "Blue as robin's eggs, but more importantly they are inquisitive and intelligent and filled with a hint of sly laughter." Eyes stay young much longer than any other part of a person, and her eyes were still inquisitive and intelligent. He had loved her hair as well and forbade her to ever cut it, so she braided it into the usual long braid and let it stream down her back.

Michael. The diary mentions a Michael. MT. Should she go back to Mrs. Bemis she wondered? How much would she remember about a guy named Michael? Linda went back to the diary and read a passage that referred to Michael. "Just a little something I organize."

Well that's a clue. Michael was an organizer of something at a time when the campus climate was in turmoil. The flower girl describes him as a forceful personality. Maybe she didn't need Mrs. Bemis. Maybe the answer was in the archives.

Greenbriar Library had a very thorough archive system. The staff had gone painstakingly through all of the available campus newsletters and created digitized versions of them. Linda could access them via her home computer.

Linda had arrived at Greenbriar in the Fall of 1970. She remembered that the campus was still reeling from a student strike against the war in Viet Nam. And she remembers the ruins of the old hall that had been burned by an arsonist. "Michael. A fire. Revolt." A good place to start.

She typed 1970-71 into the search dialog box and was greeted with 10 issues from that year. She switched to her web browser and typed in "Greenbriar building burns in war protest," and a wiki article came up. May. It happened in May. She went back to the archives and skimmed through the articles until she found a likely target: May 14, 1970.

She smiled just a little as she noticed the newspaper's logo. The large header was designed in a very sixties style font, psychedelic like the lettering on The Beatles *Rubber Soul* Album. Happenings. Cute. But her eyes moved quickly to the title story. "On Strike: Greenbriar Joins the Movement," by Michael Thompson

Eureka! Maybe this is THE Michael. She read the first paragraph.

"Students and faculty members at Greenbriar joined thousands of others on campuses across the country in the national strike against the war in Southeast Asia, university complicity with the military, and repression of political dissent."

She scanned the rest of the paper. There was a picture of the building burning and images of the strikers. The leader of the students was not Michael, but as she scanned the article she came across another reference: *Campus Editor Michael Thompson spoke out against the war and called for renewed opposition to the ROTC program.*

It wasn't hard to track down Michael Thompson. A man of that name who had graduated in 1970 showed up. He had become a successful lawyer and author, and his bio listed his alma mater as Greenbriar. There was a phone number on his webpage, but Linda decided to make the first contact through email.

Dear Mr. Thompson,

My name is Linda Harner Metzner. We have never met, but we were both at Greenbriar College around the same time. I was an adjunct in 1970, the term after you graduated.

You might remember my husband, Dr. Alex Metzner?

Alex passed away this year, and I have returned to Greenbriar and bought the house that we lived in. Your name has come up in regards to a girl student at the college who used to occupy the house, and I was wondering if I could call and ask you a few questions? I know it has been a long time, and I don't have much information to go on but maybe, if I were able to give you a little information, it might jog your memory as to this girl's identity.

If you think you can be of help, please call me at 802-349-9409. Thank you, Linda

She pressed "send" and released a sigh. Well, now all she could do was wait. She didn't know if she'd have the nerve to just cold call him but, if her other leads didn't pan out, it might come to that.

Suddenly, it was all too much. Linda's mind was weighed down and everything started to blend together. She realized that she had been so determined to solve the mysteries of the flower girl that she had not really spent any time exploring Greenbriar. She opened the door and tested the temperature. It was breezy enough for a light layer, so slipped into her blue jean jacket, which made her feel adventurous and young, and headed down Market Street.

So much about the town hadn't changed. It was an old New England village where the stately 19th century two-story Victorians remained much as they always had, and the manicured lawns rolled down from the gentle hills to the street unchanged by development. A lump rose in Linda's throat as she remembered the impact this town had had on her. She had received her degrees from New York State schools, urban buildings in the middle of the

Big Apple. Busy, exciting, but not soothing. When she had been accepted as an adjunct at Greenbriar, she couldn't believe her luck. This was the life she had always dreamed of, the life that was different from the two-bedroom flat in New Jersey without a backyard.

She strolled on down to the campus, preparing herself. It was just as she remembered, and her eyes watered with the memories. Her life had been spent mainly in the Language and Lit building and it was still there, right in the same place. It was a Saturday, so she indulged herself with a walk through the empty halls. The floors had been redone, but otherwise it looked much the same. The upstairs, where her had office had been, was closed off. She wondered if the adjuncts still hung out there and compared notes, working into the night simultaneously grading papers and working on their dissertations.

She remembered the two Pete's, John Peterson and Don Peterson. John was a TA in Math and Don in History. They had made her laugh and when the building was being locked behind them they had headed down to a little bar. What was it called? Jon's? Jerry's? Jillian's? She didn't really remember, but it was the only bar open into the wee hours, and they unwound by griping about their respective lots, the deadlines, the lazy students, the demanding professors, and of course, their sense of subjugation as nobodies. But they both knew that someday they would be through it and one of the elite themselves. Of course, they promised that they would be much kinder and thoughtful and not the least bit snobby. And then they would laugh.

She had lost contact with Pete and Pete and wondered where they had ended up. She walked down the stairs and into the corresponding descending darkness and out into the quad. So still. So open and empty as if it all had never really happened. *Oh Alex, I wish you were here. There is so much I want to ask you, so much I want to know.*

Consecration Hall. She had never seen it. It had burned down the year before her arrival. The protests against that war had continued for a few years, but she had never been involved. She had heard the stories. Kent State. Collective protests around the country. It had been a turbulent time. And the flower girl was caught up in it somehow.

Chapter Eleven

The Girls Go To Montreal

Dear Diary,
I know I am supposed to write about things here that I can't say other places. All the secrets of my heart. But I feel that putting it down on paper will ruin the magic. Is it love? Is it the excitement of the forbidden? By writing it down I may lose it. I haven't told it here, just held it in my heart where matters of the heart are meant to be. But what will he think when I tell him?

Dear Diary,
Sylvie grabbed me in the hall. We're organizing!

Come! Tonight! I guess there is a protest against the fact that women have curfews on campus and men don't. They plan to march on City Hall. Greenbriar needs to have its own women's health program - the one at the state department is too far away and too insufficient. I don't know. Sylvie is such a whirlwind - I am overwhelmed and enthralled by her. Maybe. Maybe I will go.

Dear Diary,
Sylvie said she was goaded into her feminist activism when Professor Coate suggested he sit on his lap during his office hours. Professor Coate! But he is ancient! You could see it really enraged her. Her mouth tightened and her eyes were like flames. What a creep, she spat out. Men have all the power, she said. We need to fight back. But it is different isn't it dear diary, when two people love each other. Isn't it?

Linda rose early and walked in the peaceful silence of the Greenbriar campus. So little of her life spent here, so much of her development. This little haven of history where stone buildings and white spires nestled against green mountains, where red brick shops line the busy main street filled with tourists and students. So placid now. She tried to see it as it was, before she came, when 400 million college students erupted across the nation in protest.

She had been in college then, but her campus had been relatively quiet. She hadn't taken part in any demonstrations.

She tried to envision it. Mobs of people with anti-war signs lining the quad. Alex had never said much about. *It was a crazy time, he had said. There was plenty of activism here, but the college didn't close down completely after the post-Kent State riots like some did. It was a relief when it was all over and we could just start educating kids again.*

Linda tried to picture the flower girl, not knowing at all what she might have looked like. Michael Thompson. All there on the quad, holding signs, chanting *"Hell no, we won't go"* and *"Hey, hey LBJ, how many kids did you kill today?"* It made her feel like such a child. She had known boys, too soon become men, who had not come back and those who had come back different people. But she had never been tested to stand up against anything. Would she have risked getting expelled or thrown into jail to stand up for what she believed in? Maybe the flower girl is me, she thought. Timid, a good girl, a sidelines girl.

When she was nineteen, a favorite professor had given her a lift home and, as she turned to thank him, he slid his hand into the gap of her sundress and cupped her breast.

She remembers freezing. Panicked. She hadn't really known what to do. But the gesture had been a question and when his question was answered by startled eyes and trembling lips he withdrew. "You aren't that kind of girl," he had said.

But I liked him. He was young and handsome. If he had continued, would I have had the will to stop him? If he had tried to barter for my grade in class, would I have capitulated? There were other advances from other men after that, but none by a man with power over her. She thought about Alex. He was a professor, and she had been an adjunct, but she was over 21. There was never a hint of forcefulness on his part - only respect and kindness. Always. But she couldn't help but remember, as she gazed at the sun just above the horizon blanketing this historic campus with a soft gauze of light, all those young girls gathered around him with their short skirts and eager smiles. She had to wonder if Alex had ever invited one or two to sit on his lap. She hadn't considered it before. Alex would never have done that. But Larry might have.

Linda bided her time at the Green City Diner until nine o'clock when the antique store opened. She had seen it in the window - a brocade settee that would fit nicely into the window alcove on the second floor. It looked just like one that had been there when she and Alex had first set up house-keeping. As she walked into the shop, she was greeted by a trim, energetic woman in her seventies. "Hello! May I help you" she smiled.

"Good morning. Yes, I am interested in that

settee that you have in the window. I just moved into the old Turner house on Minot Street. My husband and I lived there many years ago, and I have just bought it back."

"Oh how wonderful! It is such a lovely old house. You and your husband must be happy to be able to live there again."

"Well, sadly my husband, Alex, died just this year. When I found out that house was available I jumped on it. I have happy memories of this place."

"I am so sorry," she said with true sympathy. "Did I know him? I have lived here all of my life and I used to be Postmistress. I knew just about everyone - at least by their mailing addresses," she smiled.

"I apologize, I should have introduced myself. I am Linda Harner Metzner and my husband was Alex Metzner. He was an English professor at Greenbriar College."

"And I am Hattie Miller. That name does ring a bell. Well, I am certainly sorry that you have to come back to us under such circumstances. But, let's take a look at the settee and see if it will provide you some cheer."

The small sofa was in perfect condition. Its mauve brocade shimmered slightly against the dark walnut trim.

"This isn't a real antique, you know, if that is what you are wanting. It is a reproduction of an

18th century style couch done by a local woodworker named Jamie Caldor. He lives here in town. But it is so realistic, I just had to put it in my window."

'It's beautiful, and I don't really care if it is an antique. Hopefully, that means it doesn't have an antique price tag."

She laughed. "You are quite right about that. An original would cost you about $8000, but Jamie would probably let this go for about $3000."

That was still a lot for her, but the sale of the house in Pennsylvania had given her some equity to burn, so she decided to buy it.

"Wonderful!" Hattie said. "Jamie likes to deliver his furniture himself. Can you fill out this form with your name, address and phone? He will give you a call."

Linda paid for the couch, filled out the form, and said goodbye, promising to come back when she had more leisure and spend some time looking around her shop. She spent another hour picking up a few groceries and garden implements and had just arrived home when the call arrived.

"Mrs. Metzner? This is Jamie Caldor. I have been informed that you have purchased one of my sofas?"

"Oh, Mr. Caldor! Yes, I have. It is beautiful. You do wonderful work."

"Please, call me Jamie. When is a good time for me to drop it by? Are you free this afternoon?"

"And you can call me Linda. Yes, as a matter

of fact, I have just finished all my errands and will be home. Let me warn you though, the room is on the second floor. I probably can't get it up there myself. Would you be able to take it up the stairs?"

"I will bring Andy along - he is my assistant. The two of us can get this little thing up any set of stairs." Then he laughed. "Is it a spiral staircase?"

Linda chuckled. "No, I wouldn't do that to you. It is just a plain staircase with an L-shape at the bottom. It's a main staircase and very wide."

"Sounds great! How does 3:30 pm strike you?"

"That is fine. I will be looking forward to it."

Linda put away the groceries and settled the new spade and rake into the garden shed.

She wandered up to the alcove to look at the empty space. She smiled ruefully. *I didn't measure this space.* But she knew it would fit. Something about it just fit, in every way.

At 3:30 the doorbell rang, and she opened it to let the two men inside.

"Mrs. Metzner - er, Linda, I'm Jamie Caldor," he said with a friendly grin and an outstretched hand.

"Hi Jamie." She smiled back. He was a pleasant looking man with slightly graying hair and bright blue eyes. His square jaw radiated a quiet strength, and his tanned skin indicated time spent in the sun. His hand was calloused and his grip firm.

This is a working man.

He turned to the man behind him, a much younger man, maybe 25, with broad shoulders. "This is Andy. If we can't get that little couch upstairs between the two of us, no one can." He grinned.

Linda laughed. "I believe it. Will it fit through this doorway? I am sorry, but I bought this on a whim and did not check measurements."

"Well, that's our job." Jamie pulled out the tape measure that was clipped to his belt.

"36 inches. Plenty of room." He did the same for the stairwell, calculating for movement about the L-shape and nodded. "We're good."

"You had better check the alcove too. I am keeping it anyway, but before you trek up the stairs you might want to see if it will fit up there."

The tape measure affirmed that the settee would fit as comfortably as Linda intended it to.

"This piece is really more awkward than it is heavy," Jamie said. "A little careful maneuvering and we will have it up there in minutes."

And that is exactly what it took. The two burly men lifted the piece of delicate furniture and, being careful of the curled legs and arched top, installed in carefully on the hardwood floor.

The back of the settee fit perfectly so that one could see out of the windows onto the lawn, and the arms flared ever so gently, matching the slant of the alcove walls.

Something in Linda's heart swelled as she saw it there. It seemed so like the one she and Alex and owned so long ago. For the first time, she began to feel as if she had really come home.

Andy had immediately gone downstairs, but Jamie stood watching her with a softness in his eyes and a slight smile.

"This means something to you." Not a question. A simple statement.

"Yes." Linda didn't say anything else but it was as if he knew there was nothing else that needed to be said.

"Well, that means something to me. I have always tried to build my furniture with people in mind. Special pieces can comfort us with their beauty. I am glad when I provide people with more than just a place to sit or dine."

Linda looked at him with a mischievous smile. "Did you major in Woodworking and minor in Philosophy?"

Jamie laughed. "I lasted two years at Greenbriar before I realized I didn't need a college education to do what I wanted to do. But I am glad I went and sometimes am sorry I didn't finish. You?"

"Oh, yes. I finished. I did some adjunct teaching there while writing my dissertation. The last forty years have been spent teaching English Literature at a small college in Pennsylvania. My husband was an English Professor as well. At Penn State."

"Ah yes, I am sorry. Hattie told me you were

recently widowed."

Linda turned to look at the settee and let out a deep sigh. "Yes. Alex and I lived in this house and had a settee just like this. Seems like a hundred years ago and like yesterday all at the same time."

"I lost my wife a few years ago," he said quietly. "It takes awhile to move on. It is both comforting and difficult to stay put where you both spent so many happy years. But, one does move on. If you need anything, just call."

Linda looked directly into his eyes and saw his genuine kindness and concern.

She smiled. "Thank you, I will."

The day had been so busy that Linda had not had any time to think about the flower girl since early that morning. The house was so still. The arrival of the settee had made it seem like home, and she began to think that maybe it would all go away. Maybe the flower girl would leave now that she had told her that Alex was Larry.

But then she shook her head as if to clear out the cobwebs. But no, no, there is something more. Maybe revealing that secret was just to get her attention. There was something else the flower girl wanted her to know.

She fell asleep that night so easily, so peacefully. She had gotten to the point where she did not worry about being wakened.

Maybe it was that relaxation that made that night different. The music came. But so did an image.

A sweet lilting tune aroused her to consciousness and she saw her. A young female shape, light, with long hair. She held a guitar and sang as if to the moon. Linda reached over and started the recorder on her tablet. She listened without trying to understand; instead, she drank in the vision and when it was through, went back to sleep.

When the light came though her window, she had almost forgotten about the song. Instead of the trepidation she usually felt, she felt calm eagerness to hear what the flower girl had left for her. She sat on the new settee with her coffee, found the new recording and listened. Lovely folksy melody:

The sky fades into streaks of blue
You can hear the shadows call.
The boys try out for the football team
And the girls go to Montreal.
There's someone there to welcome you.
He believes in health for all.
When they reach out he tries to help
The girls who come to Montreal.
Some girls get married,
And some girls risk it all
In alleys dark and dangerous,
But some go to Montreal.
He survived the Nazi Prison camps
To Canada he came.
He was attacked and vilified.

People cursed his name.
The sky fades into streaks of blue
And the evening shadows call.
The boys pledge their fraternities,
And the girls go to Montreal.
Some girls get married,
And some girls risk it all
In alleys dark and dangerous,
But some go to Montreal.

The girls go to Montreal?

Chapter 12

Sylvie

The perennial beds had been quite neglected, and three hours on her hands and knees clearing the thatch and trimming deadwood made the ground ready for winter. Gardening also was a good way for Linda to clear her head and, as she raked, the lilting tune of "the girls go to Montreal" played in her head. She had a sense that she knew this story and keywords jumped out at her: Nazi, health, vilified. Finding out who this man was would be necessary to understanding what the flower girl was trying to tell her.

"Oh," she groaned as she straightened up and arched her back. "I am not in shape for this." So, she didn't mind at all when she heard her phone's ringtone from where she had laid it on the patio table.

She peeled off her gloves and wiped her hands on the backside of her pants.

"Hello? This is Linda Metzner."

"Mrs. Metzner? Hello. This is Michael Thompson."

"Michael! Thanks so much for getting back to me. I hope that my request wasn't a bother for you."

"Not at all. I remember Dr. Metzner well, and am sorry to hear of his passing. You seem to have a question that you hope I can help you with. Something about a student who used to live in your house?"

"Yes. Yes. I am not at liberty to explain why, but I need to find out her identity. I uncovered a diary that I believe belonged to her and she mentions a Michael who steered her to safety during the Consecration Hall fire. He seemed to be an activist, and I ran across your name when reading old copies of the school paper. You were an organizer on campus?"

"Yes, I was. I remember that fire well, of course. But as for the girl - can you give me anything else to go on? I knew a lot of girls in college," he laughed.

"Quite understandable," she smiled. "Well she mentioned she was from Montana. She also mentioned someone named Sylvie, who it seems was also an organizer."

"Ah, yes, Sylvie Blake. She was something. Pretty much single-handedly built the women's rights movement on campus. Montana? Sorry, doesn't ring a bell. What house are we talking about? The old Victorian on Minot Street? I seem to remember that Dr. Metzner bought that house when he came to Greenbriar. He held some great informal study sessions there."

"Yes, that's the one."

"I left Greenbriar and went straight to law school, and I don't remember anyone else living there but Dr. Metzner."

"Well, thanks for your time. Would you happen to know how I can get hold of Sylvie Blake?"

"I heard that she had continued with her social activism, but I don't know where. You could probably check with alumni services."

"Good idea."

"Good luck. Sorry I couldn't help."

As she ended the call Linda felt slightly cheered because now she could at least follow up on Sylvie who seemed to have been a great influence on the flower girl.

After a brisk shower to hose off the garden dirt, Linda poured herself a glass of Merlot and headed toward her favorite rattan chair in the corner of the sunroom with the diary. It was Friday afternoon and the alumni office would be closed, so she thought perhaps a good place to start would be to locate every entry that mentioned Sylvie by name. Perhaps she could isolate some helpful information.

As often was the case, it was a frustrating read. There was no real sense of organization - no dates for instance. The large, loopy writing was often hard to decipher and she had written in pencil. Years of storage had almost erased certain portions of the text. After a long while, she was tempted to give up for the evening, but then something caught her eye. Yes, there it was: Sylvie.

As the sunlight was beginning to fade, she moved the reading lamp and held the diary close to its glow.

I went to see Sylvie about it. I am frozen. My mind won't work. Mr. B says I should ask Sylvie. That she can help me. She was so kind and understanding. She asked me who, and I said I couldn't say. She didn't press me. She just said I should go see someone named Morgan Taller. That he could help me. She would give me all of the information.

So, the flower girl was worried about something. Morgan Taller. She sighed. "Well, nothing like one more name to locate."

She stared off into the distance as the last of the sun melted into the horizon. So much was twirling around in her brain. Melodies and images combined like some surreal modern Monet video. She blinked and shook her head as she heard the doorbell.

"Mr. Caldor?" She said in surprise.

"Jamie, remember?" he said with a smile.

"Of course," she laughed. "To what do I owe the pleasure?"

"I just thought I would stop by to see if the settee was still to your satisfaction. I offer a 30-day money back guarantee. Maybe on second glance you feel that it doesn't quite fit the space as you had hoped."

"My goodness. That is quite impressive. No, actually I love it. I was just looking at it today and thinking that I couldn't have found a more perfect piece."

"Oh, well, then. That's great. So. . ." He put his hands in his pockets with a sort of nervous energy. "Since I am here, might I take you for a drink somewhere? Welcome you to the neighborhood?"

Linda froze for a moment. Ah, the ulterior motive. It had been a long time. She wasn't sure that she was ready.

"Oh Jamie that is so nice of you. But, I think I will have to take a rain check. I am in the middle of some important research and I think if I don't finish it tonight I run the risk of losing it all together." She smiled and knocked the heel of her hand against her temple a couple of times. "As I age it seems that things don't stay in here as long as they used to."

He gave her a small, somewhat shy, grin. "I understand. Pretty short notice. Hey, maybe I will give you a call sometime and we can set something up that works for you?"

"Yes, that would be fine." She figured she might be able to prepare herself for dating again, given a little time to think about it.

He nodded and turned to go. But then he glanced back over his shoulder and winked. "Age? You don't look too much older than a Greenbriar co-ed."

Linda said goodbye with only a slight upturn of her lips to indicate she understood. Those eyes. Yes, honest, warm sincere. She would treat him better next time. She shut the door and leaned back against it with a sigh.

What now? It was too early for bed and really hard for her to wait until the alumni office opened on Monday.

Her computer had been off all day, so she brought it to life and waited for the "ding" that indicated it was firing up. What to look for was the question.

She went back to the song lyrics. *Let's try this*. She typed "Montreal + Nazi prison camp +

healthcare" into the search box. She skimmed through the results of five pages and nothing registered. Ok, she thought. Maybe some different wording is needed: "Holocaust survivor" + Montreal + Health." Again, nothing.

Ok, one more try. Montreal is important of course. The song mentions the exact words "Nazi prison camp" so let's try that. And maybe something more specific than health. Who cares about health. A doctor? She typed "Montreal + Nazi prison camp" + doctor" into the search box and began to scan the results.

She was reading down the titles of the entries of the third page when something caught her eye. Henry Morgentaler, 90, dies. Abortion Defender in Canada.

Dr. Morgentaler moved to Canada in 1950, finished medical school at the University of Montreal in 1953, and for 15 years practiced general medicine in a working-class district of Montreal.

Morgentaler. Morgan Taller.

Chapter Thirteen

The Abortion Underground

The autumn nights come early in Vermont. Linda drew her blanket around her, and as she tossed and turned in and out of sleep she saw faces. She was there. The fire at Consecration Hall. People yelling. No more war. She saw Carl. She had not thought about Carl for a long while. She had been his TA in New York. His image swirled and there he was in a military uniform - goodbye Miss Harner - I'll be back. I know, she smiled. Be careful. Then he began to cry and his uniform dissolved. Carl! She cried, come back! And the hall burned, and she was grabbed from behind. I'm Michael, he said. You can trust me. It is time for anarchy. The war is a farce. And the flower girl sang, like some modern-day Nero, as the fire raged. Alex! Larry? His face drew near and he kissed her and said there is nothing for me here.

Linda spent the weekend researching everything she could find about Henry Morgentaler and Sylvie Blake.

It turned out that neither was hard to find. Morgentaler was famous for his abortion clinic that he opened in Montreal in 1968 and was a tireless advocate for the right of women to choose. He was a Holocaust survivor who felt it his duty and obligation to help those in need. Even after the Canadian judiciary ruled that three qualified physicians must deem an abortion necessary, Dr. Morgentaler continued to perform them on demand. Before the Roe vs. Wade decision in the United States in 1973, it wasn't uncommon for American girls to head to Montreal to Morgentaler's clinic.

Sylvie Blake was a known activist who championed women's issues on campus and, according to the Greenbriar website, helped to make arrangements for girls who wished to have an abortion to go to Dr. M's clinic. It was dubbed the abortion underground.

Blake was just as easy to find as Morgentaler. Since she left Greenbriar, she had gone on to graduate school and then on to high positions in industry and politics. Linda typed a message into Sylvie's website contact page, but thought that come Monday she would see if there was an address and phone on file she could access. Sylvie had known the flower girl and it seems had been an important influence on her. Michael may have been just a passing presence and the flower girl just another girl to him, but Sylvie - she had a feeling that important things had transpired between the flower girl and Sylvie. Perhaps she had finally found the connection she needed.

Linda busied herself throughout the week-end, scrubbing, cleaning, polishing. Her hands needed to stay busy to keep up with her mind.

Maybe I should call Maureen. She might remember Sylvie.

But she felt she needed to tackle this alone. Even if Maureen remembered Sylvie, Linda doubt-ed that she would have any more information than what she had already found on Sylvie's website. No, it was important to talk with Sylvie because what she wanted to know wasn't about her, what she wanted was the identity of her ghostly friend.

She hoped that she might receive a quick reply from Sylvie but when no email came, she headed to the Alumni Office. The girl who was at the desk was obviously a student and she smiled politely when Linda arrived. "Good morning. I'm Meghan. How can I help you?"

"I was wondering if there is system in place

for alumni of Greenbriar to contact each other. Some kind of reciprocal database?"

"Well, we keep records of all the alumni who request it, but we don't have records of everyone. What years are we looking at?"

"I would say 1968 - 1972."

"What is the name you are looking for?"

"Sylvie Blake. I think she may have graduated in 70 or 71."

Meghan quickly pecked away at her keyboard. "Yes, we have a Sylvie Blake. She seems to be an alumni donor and has stayed active in Greenbriar affairs."

"Is it possible to get a phone number?"

Meghan scanned the monitor. "Her records indicate that she is open to being contacted by other Greenbriar alumni and faculty. Do you have some ID with you."

After Meghan had checked her ID and verified her name in the faculty database, Linda left the office with two phone numbers in her hand: Sylvie Blake's office and cell phone numbers.

Now, the question is will I have the courage to contact her?

She thought carefully about what she would say. *What can I say that will jog her memory - how can I describe the flower girl so that Sylvie might remember her?*

"Hello. This is Sylvie Blake." The voice was pleasant and strong.

"Hi!" I said with much less strength. "My name is Linda Metzner. I was an adjunct professor at Greenbriar College in 1971. I believe you attended Greenbriar?"

"Why yes I did. Are you any relation to Dr. Alex Metzner? He taught at Greenbriar when I was there."

"In a way, yes. I married him."

She laughed "Well, that's related enough. How is Alex?"

Linda gave her the information of his death and about coming back to live in their old house.

"Oh, I am sorry to hear that. I never took a class from him, but he was a good teacher from what I heard. What can I do for you?"

She dove in. "Well, I know this was a long time ago, but I am trying to find out some information about a girl who was a student at Greenbriar at the time you were here. I also would love to get some information about your activism. I understand you led the movement for women's healthcare and other issues."

"Boy, that was such a time wasn't it? Through the lens of our present day it is hard to believe what went on back then. Yes, I advocated for equality for women on campus.

"Watched over us like hawks they did. The boys - well they did what they wanted, but if a girl missed curfew, watch out! And there was no help for women as far as health was concerned. We had to go to the county doctor. And free access to birth control? Ha. Non-existent."

This gave Linda the lead-in she wanted. "Well, I know you seemed to be very influential on young women at the time. The reason I am calling you is because I have found a diary of a young woman in our house. There is no name on the diary, but in one entry she mentions you. She seems to have been very impressed by you. I am hoping you can help me identify her. I would like to be able to return the diary to her as it contains some great stories and I am sure she would love to have it. *What's one more lie. I am getting used to it.*

"Well, that is nice to hear, but I don't know how I can possibly remember her. Can you give me any other hints?"

She took a deep breath. "Well, I also understand that one of your causes was to help girls obtain abortions in Canada."

She didn't even pause. "Yes, that is common knowledge now. You must remember how it was before Roe v Wade. The system favored men, and for a girl to get pregnant – well it damaged her future. She often had to drop out of college and of course the parents weren't happy. The boys, of course, denied it."

"Can you tell me a little about it?"

"Well there was a doctor in Montreal named Morgentaler." She continued to tell Linda what she had already learned about him. "What I would do was to help the girls make contact with him and arrange transportation and lodging for them. I would give them support in getting any excuse from classes that they might need."

"Did you do a lot of these? I mean, would you be able to remember the girls you helped? You see, I think the girl whose diary I found may be one of them."

"Oh, I see. Yes, I think I might. I took it very seriously and spent a lot of time with each girl. They needed a lot of support when they decided to undertake this. Would you know anything else about the girl? What year do you think?"

"I believe it might have been 1971."

"Yes, Morgentaler was still performing abortions then - illegally of course. But I knew he was a good doctor - very conscientious - unlike the illegal back alley stuff the girls would have received in the states. I was about ready to graduate and there weren't as many then. Anything else to go on?"

So Linda took a chance. "I think she was a singer. With long blond hair." I stopped. "She mentions her hair in the diary. She was a songwriter too I think."

"Oh, that would be Holly! Holly McNab. She was such a sweet thing. And yes, a wonderful singer and songwriter. So, she lived in your house?"

Sylvie paused. "I guess she must have come back to Greenbriar after I graduated. You see, she never came back from Montreal. I contacted Dr. Morgentaler, and he said she never showed. I didn't know what had become of her. I figured she must have changed her mind and gone home to have the baby. Or maybe it turned out she wasn't pregnant. Girls sometimes got prematurely worried and imagined they were when they weren't. But given that she did not come back, I doubt that was true in this case."

Linda was silent a moment as she let that sink in.

"Did she ever mention who the father was?"

"No, and I never asked. But I do remember that she was quite taken with a few men on campus. Michael Thompson was one. And someone she called Monsieur B."

Chapter 14

The Rain Has Stopped

Linda woke to the sound of the rain. Whipped by a wild wind, it beat upon the roof and against the windows like all the furies had been unleashed into the deep chasm of the night sky. She turned to glance at the clock only to find it as blank as the night.

Oh crap. Power outage. She reached for the flashlight that she always kept by her bed and walked through the house quickly, making sure that all of the windows were securely fastened and the doors tightly locked. *Glad I took the time to get wood last week. At last I will be warm.*

She carefully layered newspaper and kindling in the small cast iron stove in the living room, adding larger logs as the flames grew.

What do I do next? Who was Holly McNab? The next step would be to locate her in the school database, but somehow her heart just wasn't in it. The threads that were knitting themselves together seemed oppressive. *What is it you want from me, young Holly? Did you have a child? Who is Monsieur B? Oh, too many questions, and too much of a burden. I didn't come back for this.*

Linda spoke aloud "So, now what? Is it this secret that you wanted me to find? Will you give me something more to go on?

She must have dozed off, and when she woke the fire had burnt down to cinders. The rain had stopped and in exchange for the relentless noise, there was an equally relentless quiet. No clocks ticking, no refrigerator humming. And then, seeping through the quiet like mist upon an ocean, she heard a soft guitar. Holly. She quickly reached for her phone and pressed record.

It's been raining in these hills
For such a long time.
Can't remember when I last saw the sun.
Tears upon stone, we've been resting here alone
And waiting and waiting.
One day we enter this life screaming.

We are named, we live, and then we die.
And it is that about our birth,
That lingers on the earth
When we are gone, when we are gone.
Please give me a name,
So that I can find some peace
And those I've left behind
Will know what's become of me.
Please tell my momma to come and see me
So she can lay a flower on my grave.
She can kneel and pray,
And know I didn't run away
From what she taught me,
From all she taught me.
Please give me a name,
So that I can find some peace
And those I've left behind
Will know what's become of me.
When I hear her sweet voice talk to me gently
I will know that the rain has finally stopped.
I want her to know that I don't lie here alone
And that I'm sorry, I'm sorry.
It's been raining in these hills
For such a long time.
Can't remember when I last saw the sun.
Tears upon stone, we've been resting here alone
And waiting and waiting.

Please give me a name. *Is that what you want*
Holly? Just for someone to identify you? I will

145

listen again when I am more rested.

The sun was breaking through the clouds, and it was clear that the deluge the night before had done some damage. Tree limbs were scattered upon the lawn, and the electric company's vehicles were forming a parade out on the street. It would be a while before the power came on. She pulled on jeans and a sweatshirt, wiggled into her boots, and went outside to assess the damage.

The high winds had ripped off a couple of the shutters, and a gutter was hanging precariously from the center gable. *Oh, no!* There was a very ominous dark patch on the roof. She hoped it didn't correlate with a prodigious cascade of water on the inside.

It took a couple of days for the electricity to come back throughout the town. In the meantime, Linda spent time cleaning up the debris and assessing the damage. It became clear that she would need to hire a carpenter to do some repairs.

She made some phone calls, but it was evident that everyone else in town had the same idea, and no one seemed to be available. She really wanted to have someone look at this soon. It was an old house and rot might set in very quickly.

"Hey!" She heard a masculine voice behind her. "You ok? I thought I would check in - it was a pretty powerful storm. Suffer any damage?" It was Jamie Caldor.

"Hello yourself. Boy, are you a sight for sore

eyes! You don't do general handyman stuff do you? It looks like I could use some shutters repaired. And I think I have some leaking inside the walls. Probably need to remove some plaster and replace some baseboards."

He pursed his lips and crossed his arms as if considering deeply what she had just said. Then he broke out in a grin. "Sure. Point me at 'em."

She liked having him there. There was warmth in his presence as he went about the place. He moved from the ladder to his truck with an agile grace, and he certainly knew what he was doing.

"Would you like to take a lunch break?" she asked. " I made plenty of soup and some freshly baked bread."

"A man would be an idiot to turn that down," he said cheerfully.

He dug in with the appetite of one who had been burning calories in a big way.

"How are things at your place," she asked.

"No real damage. I reinforced my house pretty well after the last big storm we had a couple of years ago. However, I do expect plenty of erosion near my creek. The ground around there is fairly soft, and there is no vegetation to hold it back. Last storm I lost half of the creek bank."

It took him two days and, as he packed up his gear, she followed him to his truck.

"I can't thank you enough" she said. "I'll bet that you really don't do much of this kind of thing on a professional basis. You are an artist. Send me a bill, please."

He smiled. "Artists all start somewhere. I am happy to help. No charge. Heck, the soup and bread were payment enough. See it as one neighbor helping another."

He paused a moment. "Linda, I know we don't know each other well, and I don't mean to be presumptuous, but I sense there is something bothering you. If you ever want to talk, let me know. I have broad shoulders and am a good listener."

She swallowed and turned her head away slightly before looking back. "Thank you," she said quietly. "Yes, there is something, but I have to deal with it myself."

"Well, when you are ready I'm here."

"Yes," She smiled. "Yes, I think I know that."

It wasn't until the next morning that something he had said crept back into her mind.

Erosion. Lost half of my creek bank.

The day was bright and cloudless and so she pulled on her rubber boots and shrugged into her wool shirt. She tied back her hair and knew where she had to go.

The gravestone had been perched on the edge of a soft cliff that looked as if it had withstood many a rainstorm, but she remembered how precarious it had seemed. The high grass grew around but otherwise there was no vegetation.

She approached the area with a foreboding. She didn't know why. She had no idea what to expect. The rain had hit that area hard, and the grass had flattened completely. All that was left was mud and debris. She carefully approached the stone, having to watch her footing. At least two feet of the promontory had given in. Where she expected the stone to be was covered with a large branch.

She gingerly moved the branch aside. The stone seemed larger because the soil and grass around it had been washed away. It lay slightly askew and, as she bent down to examine it, she realized that before this she had only seen part of the stone. She now saw the stone in its entirety. Just below the small flower was an inscription:

Mother and Child.

Chapter Fifteen

Digging Up The Past

"Should I turn to Maureen?" she thought as she slowly stripped off her wet boots and pulled the stocking cap from her head.

She put a cup of the morning's coffee into the microwave. *Heavy on the cream and sugar. I need it.*

It hadn't really dawned on her until then - *I have a body buried in my back yard. I guess I had been able to pretend that it was just a stone - that there was nothing there beneath. Should I tell the town about it? I guess there might be dead bodies buried all over a state this old, but this stone is fairly new. Maybe it needs to be moved to a cemetery? Or exhumed and examined? Could they even find out anything after 40 years?*

She finished the hot coffee, grateful for its warmth. The caffeine seemed to help give her clarity. *Yes, I will call Maureen.*

"Hello Linda! It's been awhile since we talked. I assumed you were very busy settling in. Is everything ok? Any more from the ghost girl?"

"Hi Maureen. Yes, I am sorry that I haven't been in touch. Much going on. As far as the flower girl goes, yes there have been some surprising developments. In fact, that is why I called. Do you have some time to talk?"

"Of course. I have meetings all afternoon, but why don't we adjourn to Stella's at 5. They have a great happy hour."

"I could certainly use a happy hour," she laughed ruefully. "Ok, I will see you there."

To pass the time, she went back to the diary. Somewhere in that mass of swirls and fading pencil were some clues she had probably been over-looking - clues to the identity of the flower girl, to whether she did indeed have a lover and who he might have been. Monsieur B? Michael Thompson?

She went to where she had left the diary. It lay there on the desk in its fragility, the pages almost translucent and the pencil fading in places so that the words were sometimes not discernible. She turned the pages slowly, using her finger to underscore the lines.

Finally! Linda started to see some things she had disregarded as simple college-girl gushing.

Monsieur B said to meet him after I got out of class . . . I am so excited to see Mr. B today . . . Monsieur B is so funny . . . I don't think I have ever met anyone like M.B.

There wasn't much to go on, but the name "Monsieur B" or Mr. B did figure into the diary in an obvious way. Whether it was Holly buried out there, and whether Mr. B was the father of her child, if there was one, and if he had anything to do with the gravestone in her field - well, there was no indication. "Still lots of ifs", she sighed.

Linda was glad that Stella's was quiet that afternoon. She found a secluded table in the corner and Maureen came in just a few minutes after she had settled in.

"Maureen! It is so good to see you! Thank you for coming."

"I was so glad when I got your call. I have been thinking about you a lot, but figured you were working things out. How did you fare in the big storm?"

"Well, that is partly what I want to talk about. The storm was very revealing. Ready for a long story?"

"Hit me" she said.

Linda went from the Michael Thompson

conversation right through to Sylvie Blake. Then, she told Maureen about the storm and the discovery she had made.

"Maureen, there it was - a whole new inscription that the years had covered up. Mother and <u>Child</u>! If this is our flower girl out there - well, I just choked up. I spent all morning looking in the diary for Monsieur B and found several references - all oblique and nondescript. But he shows up often. But I wonder if it is important that we identify the father at all. Here are the words to her song."

Maureen looked at the words gravely.

"Please give me a name so that I find some peace . . tell my mother . . . I don't lie here alone."

She sighed. "It seems that what she really wants is for you to let her family know about her, and also the baby. She wants to reassure them."

"That is what I think. But I also wonder if I shouldn't tell the Sheriff's Department about the grave. I mean, even if she died of natural causes it is illegal to just bury people anywhere."

Maureen looked at her tenderly. "Linda, she has a name. Shouldn't we start calling her that?"

"I guess," she sighed. "But the threads are still tenuous, and while all directions point to her being Holly McNab, I still am not sure if the flower girl is Holly and if it is Holly who is buried out there."

"No, I guess you are right." She then nodded firmly. "Yes, tell the Sheriff. That grave needs to be dug up. Forensic people are amazing these days. They might be able to find out something from the remains. Meanwhile, I will check and see what I can find out about Holly McNab."

"Oh, Maureen, thanks so much! I am so glad I shared this with you and that you believe me."

Maureen shook her head slightly. "Linda, there are a few people in this world I would believe everything from - and you are one of them."

They spent a few minutes in companionable silence as they emptied their glasses and the rest of the cheese plate. As the day came to a close, two very reflective women left Stella's Bistro on Main Street in Greenbriar, Vermont with much on their minds.

The next morning, after another sleepless night, Linda dialed the number of the Sheriff's office.

"Good, morning, Sheriff Wallace's office," said a cheerful voice.

"Good morning. I was wondering if I could make an appointment to see the Sheriff."

"Of course. Can I say what it is about?"

"It is complicated. I think I should just explain to the Sheriff in person."

She made an appointment for the next morning, and then spent a lot of time thinking about what exactly she would tell him. She didn't think she should mention the ghost and the songs.

The next morning, she walked into the office with a firm plan. The only important thing was to find out who was buried beneath that stone.

"Good morning, Mrs. Metzner. How can I help you?"

"Good morning Sheriff Wallace. Well, I think there is a chance that someone is buried in my back field."

"A human? Why exactly do you think that?" He was professional and respectful as he took out his pen and began to take notes.

"Well, I found a gravestone. I think it has been there awhile - but I know not more than 40 years. My husband and I lived in the house from January to May 1972, and there were no grave-stones there when we left."

"When did you first find this stone, Mrs. Metzner?"

"Well, I admit, I ran across the stone when I first moved back. It was buried deep, and high grass was around it. It is very small, and all I could see was a decoration of flowers on it. I thought perhaps someone had buried a pet there. But after this last rainstorm, I went to the river to see if there was any damage to the old footbridge. The rain had caused a great deal of erosion, and I could see that there was an inscription at the bottom of the stone. It reads "Mother and Child". This made me feel that there might be some human remains under it."

He nodded as he wrote. "Yes, that seems to have been a logical conclusion on your part. I think it is probably necessary to dig and exhume this body, if there is one. Improper burial is against health rules in our area. Also, we might need to rule out foul play. It could be that someone is buried there who might actually be a missing person."

She hid her real feelings well she thought, and he didn't notice her eyes blinking rapidly and her throat throbbing. "Why, I never thought of that. How would we proceed?"

"First, I will have my crew just go do some digging. If we find something, I will have to turn it over to the County Coroner's office. When is a good time for us to come?"

"Oh, anytime."

"Let me contact the guys, and I will give you a call when we are ready to come over."

"That sounds fine," she nodded.

She went back and called Maureen. "Do you think you can come when they do this? I wouldn't like to be alone."

"Of course! I will keep my schedule and my phone free in the near future."

It didn't take long. Sheriff Wallace called the next morning. "We can be there at 2 this afternoon. That work for you?"

Linda called Maureen, and she arrived just minutes before the crew showed. They were dressed for the weather, which was slightly wet and gray, but that didn't seem to impede the crew. Four men arrived with shovels and wheelbarrows as well as some tools and rope.

"Hi ma'am. I'm Troy, and this is Bob, Ron, and Derek." We all nodded at each other politely. "We figured that there isn't a way out to this field by vehicle?"

"You figured correctly." I said. "We will need to walk down."

The ground was still somewhat wet and there were some slippery places along the way, but it didn't take long for them to reach the promontory.

Troy assessed the situation. "Until this last rain, I think this site fared pretty well. Dry. Hard soil. Lots of clay. Above the river. Probably why nothing has washed up before." He glanced at the ledge. "Also it is protected by those large rocks. Very secure place to bury a body."

He nodded at the rest of the guys and proceeded. Two of them (she didn't know which ones; she hadn't actually identified which name belonged to which man) began digging and the other two manned the wheelbarrows.

First they lifted up the stone. Even in its entirety it wasn't large - maybe 15 x 30 inches. There was nothing else revealed on the stone other than what she had already seen.

Two strong guys with shovels can do a lot very quickly in recently drenched clay.

Troy said, "Be careful. If there is a body there,

it might not be very deep below the surface - maybe just a few feet."

Slowly the men removed the earth. "I think I've found something," Bob or Ron or Derek said. They slowly lifted up a large piece of wood. Underneath the plank there appeared to be something wrapped in a soft substance that had the texture of canvas.

Troy turned to Linda. "It looks like someone, or something, might be wrapped in that tarp. I think I should call a forensic anthropologist out here. Because of the headstone, I am assuming that this is probably human. It might take awhile to get someone. Meanwhile we will fence it off, and I'll have a detail guard it until the specialist gets here."

The two women sat in silence in front of the fire until Linda said, "Well, we have to wait. If they identify a woman and child, I think we should tell them that it might be Holly McNab. Can we invent a story about why we think so?"

"You don't have to. I know how we can let them know it might be Holly."

"You found out something? About Holly McNab?"

"I have. She came to Greenbriar in 1968 and was a Junior in 1970-71. From Montana of all places. Good grades but nothing special. She stopped attending winter term."

"That is the term I came. I guess that is why our paths didn't cross. This is starting to correlate with what Sylvie told me. She went off to Montreal and never came back."

Maureen leaned forward. "Get ready. She did come back. But not until after you and Alex left. Guess where she stayed? At your house. With the Burnettes."

Chapter Sixteen

Please Tell My Mother

"Maureen! How can you possibly know that?"

"Carrie told me."

"Carrie? Your sister, Carrie? Hold on. This is getting surreal. Your sister knew the flower girl?"

I tried to remember Carrie, who was younger than Maureen and had attended Greenbriar.

"Yes. I guess she and Holly had some classes together. She remembers that Holly left one semester and just figured she had gone back to Montana. But then, she ran into Holly in town. Not too long after you and Alex left. Holly told her that she had gone home for a while, but then decided to come back and work in Greenbriar until she could save up enough money to finish her schooling. She explained that she had picked up work as a care-taker for the Burnettes who were living in your old house while he was teaching at the high school."

"No mention of a baby?"

"Carrie never knew of one. Holly seemed to be alone."

Linda sank back in her chair with a sigh. "Well, I guess that's it. We can't possibly find out anything else. I suppose Monsieur B must be Bill Burnette. Now he's dead, and there is no one else out there who can possibly give us any more information."

"Well, what now?"

"I need to go back to the lyrics of her last song and think a little bit. Hey, Maureen. Thanks. I don't know what I'd do without you."

"Feel free to call me anytime."

They hugged each other, and Linda watched as Maureen walked down the steps and into her car.

As Linda fixed herself tea she thought how repetitive things were getting. *The sun's going down and here I am in my kitchen with coffee, tea, or wine, trying to figure stuff out and wondering if music will waft in from somewhere.* She would gladly walk out the door and back to Pennsylvania if only she hadn't gotten so far into it. There was no going back now.

Linda opened up her notebook and read through the lyrics:

"I want her to know that I don't lie here alone."

Did she want her mother to know about the child?

"She can kneel and pray and know I didn't run away from all she taught me."

Pray? Her mother was religious? What might she have been taught? It didn't seem to go together - wanting her mother to know about an out-of-wedlock child but reassuring her that despite that she hadn't forsaken her principles?

Linda hadn't realized how long she had been sitting, staring blankly out of her bedroom window, until the sun was completely set.

She had a feeling that the flower girl would not return for awhile. Maybe never. *If the skeletal remains prove to be Holly's, and if I can locate her mother, maybe I have done all that she wants.*

But somehow Linda had a feeling that she would see her, and hear her, again.

Despite everything, Linda was able to have a long, restful sleep. Maybe it was because finally something was happening. Maybe the flower girl was relaxed because her story was coming out into the open, and she was passing that on to Linda indirectly somehow.

Linda occupied her time in the morning

engrossed in a good book, something she hadn't done for a long while. She looked up only when she heard her phone ring.

"Good morning Mrs.Metzner. This is Sheriff Wallace from the county police speaking. I will be coming out to the gravesite behind your house with the state forensic examiner, if that's ok."

"Of course. Will you exhume everything today?"

"We should be able to remove it all once the examiner is there to make sure any remains are unearthed in the right manner."

She once again donned her outdoor gear but felt more than capable of handling this herself without Maureen's reassuring presence.

"Mrs. Metzner, this is Dr. Sheila Carson. She is the state's forensic specialist."

"Hello Dr. Carson. Thank you for you help."

She smiled "It's my job. It sounds like an interesting case. But maybe what we will find is someone's dog buried there. If not, however, it's important to make sure the remains are removed correctly so that we might be able to identify the body."

Linda didn't say anything about her suspicions that it was Holly; she thought it best to save that until more was known.

Dr. Carson, dressed in protective gear and using gloves, very delicately removed the canvas tarp. Linda strained to see what appeared to be bones.

Dr. Carson looked up. "Yes, definitely human. Sheriff, we will need to bag these up carefully and get them back to the lab. Also, bring some soil samples along."

She looked at Linda and smiled reassuringly. "I can't promise to perform magic. This isn't a crime show. We aren't as omniscient as they make us out to be. But perhaps we can shed some light on things like gender and age, as well as the possible time of death."

Sheriff Wallace escorted me back to the house. "Thanks for bringing this to our attention Mrs. Metzner. It could be we can tie this body to a missing person's case once we find out some more information."

Linda went into the house and just sat. What now? *Wait. Yes, just wait.* But she wanted something to occupy her time.

As if on cue the doorbell rang, and there was Jamie Caldor looking somewhat awkward but sympathetic.

"A little bird told me that strange events are transpiring here. I thought maybe you could use a good meal."

She smiled. *The whole town must know.* "You know, I could. Do you know some place I might go and with whom?"

He smiled. "The Guinness Stew down at the Plough and Stars Tavern should be hot by now. And I happen to be free."

Guinness Stew was exactly what she needed. At first the conversation was about local events of the town. Jamie was very funny and was a terrific mimic.

"Well, Mrs. Smith," he said in an exaggerated New England accent. "Here at the Greenbriar General Store we give credit where credit is due, but in your case your payment is due."

They chatted amiably through dinner but when the check came, and Jamie insisted on paying it, he just looked at her as if waiting.

Linda paused just briefly and then said, "I guess there is something I should show you. Are you game?"

He nodded. "Let's go."

There was still plenty of daylight as they walked out to the promontory. The unearthed stone was lying next to the hole.

"Well. This is something. Tell me about it."

She quickly related the major specifics of finding the stone and seeing the inscription uncovered by the rain. She did not tell him about Holly.

"I decided it merited looking at by officials. Turns out these are human remains. The Forensic Anthropologist, and I guess a coroner, will be examining them."

"It wasn't here when you and your husband left the village?"

"No, I am sure it wasn't. I was out here for a walk just days before our closing. We moved away shortly after."

He knelt down and examined the stone. "This looks like local granite. It's fairly rudimentary in design. I don't think any big outfit did this carving. The police didn't want it?"

"They asked that I leave the site untouched pretty much for awhile. They might want to examine it later I guess."

We walked in silence back down hill and to the house.

"This whole thing must leave you a bit uneasy." He said. "Please know that I am here if you need anything. Anything at all."

She looked up into those very trustworthy and reassuring eyes and nodded.

After they returned, she found the file she wanted on her phone.

The sweet voice sang again,

Please tell my momma to come and see me
So she can lay a flower on my grave.

I will try Holly. I will try.

Chapter Seventeen

All That Remains

"Mrs. Metzner?"

"Yes?" Linda recognized the voice of Sheriff.

"Can you come down to my office? I have the coroner's report."

"I can be there in about an hour," she replied. "Deep breath," she told herself. "Finally, Holly. I will find out if that body out back might be yours."

She entered the building and a young officer at the front desk smiled at her. "Can I help you?"

"I am Linda Metzner. I was asked by the

Sheriff to come in."

"Oh, yes, Mrs. Metzner. He is expecting you."

"Linda! So glad you could make it on short notice."

"Well, I am pretty eager to find some answers to this whole thing. What did the coroner come up with?"

He reached for some papers on his desk and shuffled through them. "According to Dr. Carson, given the size and shape of the skeletal remains, the bodies seem to be that of a woman and a child. She can't ascertain any specific injury that may have caused death, however, all of the skeletal remains are battered slightly, which might indicate a fall. In addition, the soil samples around the body contain some algae and a little more nitrogen and potassium than the rest of the soil has. This might indicate the bodies were drowned in the river."

"I guess it doesn't matter, but was the baby a boy or a girl?"

"Gender of a baby via bone structure is almost impossible to ascertain. We might able to figure it out via bone DNA. She estimates that the bodies were placed there 30 to 50 years ago."

"Wow! And there was still enough there to examine?"

"Bones last a long time. And, I guess the quality of the tarp, in addition to the location, provided protection. There also seems to be some quicklime in the soil; it can scare off varmints as the flesh decays."

"Well, thank you. But is there anything else you can do? Something that might help identify the girl and find out why she was out there?"

"We start by looking into death records at local hospitals to see if a death of mother and child occurred. Then, we try to find out if there was a death of someone who doesn't seem to be buried anywhere. Most likely, in a case like this, we will find the result in missing persons. Cold case perhaps."

"If you find a match to a cold case or missing person, then what?"

"Well, today's science is helpful. We can actually get DNA from the bones. We can verify if the child and mother are related. Then, if we think we have a possible victim from a missing person's report, we can try to find relatives to see if we can find a DNA match."

Linda stared out the window for a moment. *To see if the mother and child are related.* She was pretty sure they were, but it wasn't something she had considered. "It is probably even harder to find the identity of the father."

He smiled ruefully. "Again, unless we have a good idea who it might be and can track him or a relative down for a DNA sample, pretty nigh impossible."

It was time.

"Sheriff, I don't know if this will help, but a friend of mine has a sister who knew a girl who lived in that house right after Alex and I left. She lived with a family called Burnette. She was named Holly McNab. She left school in 1971, but then returned quietly a year later."

"Great! That's a good place to start. I will have records look into her and see what happened to her."

He gave Linda a knowing look. "Given you seem to be smarter than the average person, I have a feeling you have more to tell me."

Linda smiled nervously. "Well, I was waiting to find out if the remains belonged to a woman. I found a diary in the house. It mentioned a woman named Sylvie and someone named Morgentaler. Through my connections here, I was able to track Sylvie down. Turns out she was a woman's activist, and Dr. Morgentaler was a doctor in Montreal famous for providing illegal but safe abortions at the time. I asked Sylvie if she remembered a girl around that time with long blond hair who was a singer. The girl mentioned these in her diary. Sylvie seems to think this is a good description of Holly McNab."

He leaned back and took a long look at Linda. "You want a job?"

She laughed. "Hardly. What I know is mostly the result of a whole lot of coincidence."

"We will get on it right away. Thanks for

your help."

That night it snowed. Linda dreamed of a blanket of white covering the open hole on the top of a promontory down by a stream. In her dream, she rose from bed and walked to the gravesite in her bare feet and white cotton nightdress. She didn't even feel the cold. The snow turned into a velvet shawl and rose from the hole. It became alive and had a girl's face and streaming hair. The girl held a baby. She felt, more than saw, a sense of anticipation and there was a question in the air. "We are almost there Holly," Linda whispered.

Linda had never had the chance to decorate the old house for Christmas. She and Alex had not lived there long enough. She decided that immersing herself in tinsel and pine might be the just the ticket to pass the time as the sheriff did his investigation.

Alex had loved Christmas. *I never had much for Christmas as a child he said. Mostly hand-me-down stuff from foster parents and I was never at a place long enough to build traditions.*

It was as if he had actually become Alex Metzner. Because of that, they had collected a variety of Christmas decorations, including a huge wreath. It was awkward to move those extra boxes, but Linda couldn't bear to part with them. Up in the attic several boxes remained unopened, and shewent to the big, flat one that she knew contained a large artificial pine wreath decorated with bells, pine cones and ribbons. It would be perfect for the front gable window. She weighed her options and decided that she didn't want to risk a sprained ankle at this juncture and knew who to call.

"Jamie? This is Linda. Hey, you said I could call you for anything?"

"Absolutely!"

"Well, I have a giant wreath in my attic that I would like to hang on my gable window. Could I coerce you into performing this gargantuan task for me?"

He laughed. "Well, I am not sure what gargantuan means, but it sounds like a piece of cake."

"Yes, I have one of those too. And coffee."

She didn't see it, but she felt his grin through the phone.

"I'm in. I have a hutch to deliver near you this afternoon. How about I come by after that? About 4:30?"

"Perfect."

He arrived right on time, and he had a ladder strapped to the top of his moving van. "I was pretty sure you wouldn't have one of these hanging around."

"And you'd be pretty sure to be right," she laughed. "Smart move."

"Yeah, I'm tall, but not that tall."

She led him upstairs to the wreath.

"I'm glad you didn't try to bring this down yourself," he said. "It is quite hefty isn't it? And awkward. But if I hold it vertically, I can get it down the stairs ok."

He maneuvered the large wreath down the attic stairs to the upper floor with the ease of someone used to moving large objects. Linda agreed. She had been smart to call him.

He had laid his bag at the bottom of the stairs and pulled out some hefty cable that he affixed to the gable overhang. He tied the wreath to the cable and left it hanging on the outside and shut the window.

"Ingenious," she said. "Now you won't have to take that thing up the ladder."

"My mother didn't have any stupid kids," he winked at her. "I've done stuff like this before. Is it ok if I put a wooden hook onto the window frame outside? Very Victorian. You won't even notice it."

"Fine with me."

Within 30 minutes, he had set up the ladder outside, climbed up and affixed the wreath to the window sash, climbed down, replaced the ladder on his van, opened the front door and said, "Now about that cake you promised me."

He dispatched it with the relish of a man who had been exerting energy. "Burnt sugar crumb cake. How did you know? My favorite cake. My wife made something like this all the time."

"Really? It was Alex's favorite cake too. Your wife and I would have probably gotten along given our propensity for choosing men who like burnt sugar crumb cake."

She realized that might have sounded provocative and tried to not blush.

But Jamie didn't react in any special way. "Yes, I think you and Grace would have liked each other. She didn't have your education, but she was a smart lady. Without any formal training at all she learned to keep the books for the business. That's how I met her. Dad hired her when she was just out of high school." He looked wistful. "I was immediately smitten."

Linda smiled. "Math? That's smart. Now, I can keep track of my basic expenses and make a monthly budget, but I am much more comfortable diagramming sentences. You must miss her."

"Of course. But one moves on. You will find that out. Grace would want me to continue to live my life. As Alex would you."

Silence set in for a moment. "More coffee?"

"Yes, please. Hey, how did that exhumation turn out?"

Linda related the details of the dig and the coroner's report. "Now, I just wait until the Sheriff does his digging. If Holly McNab turns up as a missing person he will try to locate any next of kin to see if he can find a DNA match."

"But no sign of foul play? Hole in the skull or bullet lodged in the heart? I guess I just gave away my fondness for crime drama," he laughed.

She thought it best to not give out any details so she laughed right back. "You know, I love them too. But I get the feeling that true forensics people get a little annoyed when people expect them to be detectives."

"I'm sure. But you can count on Sheriff Wallace. What he doesn't know himself, he will pass on to the right people. Hey, look at the time. I gotta fly. I get a lot of orders for custom items this time of year, and I will probably be in the shop until midnight."

"Oh, I am so sorry to have taken your valuable time for this. So thoughtless of me."

"Nonsense. All work and no cake makes Jamie a dull boy."

One more laugh together, one more look into those dependable, warm blue eyes fringed with lines that told of love and laughter but were soft with the touch of worry and sadness that comes to all who have truly lived life.

"Let me know how things turn out."

"I will. Thanks again."

As Linda closed the door behind him, she realized that just his presence there had seemed to lighten her mind.

Linda continued with her decorations. She had a real tree delivered and set up for her which she circled with lights and hung with treasured decorations that she and Alex had collected over the years. On a whim, she decided to make and frost a gingerbread house, something she hadn't done in years. Lastly, she hung both stockings on the old fireplace. Hers and Alex's. "For the memories," she whispered.

When she was through, she looked around her house with satisfaction. It was funny how something like a tradition can either make one sad or happy. In her case, her life with Alex came back as a warm memory. They hadn't had children and so they had become each other's Christmas soulmates, reveling in decorating, stuffing stockings, and searching for that one perfect present. For some reason, she didn't feel lonely. "For you Larry," she whispered. "I don't know why you loved Christmas so much. You must have been given plenty and you had a family to share it with. But maybe it helped you to become Alex - to really be your friend - to give him the life he lost and to feel for him the satisfaction of success. And I love you for that."

She was so busy that she didn't notice the time passing and she momentarily stopped worrying about whether or not the Sheriff would find the answers.

About a week passed before Linda received the call.

"Hello, Mrs. Metzner? Sheriff Wallace speaking. We located records that show Holly McNab was listed as a missing person in 1972. She never returned home from Greenbriar, and her parents were never able to locate her. We contacted her family in Montana. Her mother and one brother survive her. The brother has agreed to give us a sample of DNA. He also said he would send a picture. We should have that all by next week. Meanwhile, I think we should have a look at that diary. It might help us figure out what happened."

"Of course. But could I trade it for a copy of her photo?"

"No problem. I will make a copy and bring it to you when we get it."

With the holiday decorating behind her, that week went more slowly than the previous one but Linda filled some of it with scanning the contents of Holly's diary. She had a feeling that she wasn't quite done with it yet.

The next week, after the Sheriff had picked up the diary and handed her the photo, Linda went to her favorite chair, just next to the large window that let the early evening sun peek ever so gently, and she studied the photo. A pretty girl. Long, blond hair, sweet smile. Gorgeous brown eyes. It is interesting how rich brown eyes are so striking when accompanied by golden hair.

The test results came back in a few days. It was confirmed. The bones buried beneath the stone shared DNA with Benjamin McNab, Holly's brother.

"We've arranged for the remains to be shipped to Montana," Sheriff Wallace told her the next time he called. "I guess there is a McNab burial plot there. Mrs.McNab wants to hold a funeral for Holly, and her brother will take care of everything else."

"So, are you through?" she asked. "Do you try to go further? Find out how she died - see if there is a father of this child who should be notified?"

"Well, we will certainly give it a try. I thought we would start by putting the picture in the paper to see if anyone in town remembers her."

"That seems like a smart first step. It seems like finding folks who knew her is the only way to recreate a scene from 40 years ago. I guess one thing is obvious. Holly didn't go to Montreal. If she came back here with a baby, somebody ought to remember that."

"Like I said before," he chuckled. "You want a job?"

Linda slowly put down the phone and spoke aloud to the empty room. "Well, now your mother knows, Holly. You have a name. You are going home. This is what you wanted. Right?"

But something in her heart told her it wasn't over.

Chapter Eighteen

Mrs. Bemis Knows

It's kind of stressful always being right. This thought flashed briefly through her mind when she was awakened by the voice she had come to know so well. There was no shape this time, and the song really did seem to come out of nowhere. It was a reflex now to reach for her phone and turn on her recording app.

He's got a picture in his back pocket
Takes it with him everywhere he goes.
What is that picture in his back pocket

Only Mrs. Bemis knows.
It's five o'clock and she clears her desk,
Puts the coffee pot away for the night.
Takes one final look to see what she's missed
That's when she notices the light
Underneath his door and she hears a little giggle
When she taps and says is there more that I can do?
He replies softly you can go on home, our
Work for today is through.
He's got a picture in his back pocket
Takes it with him everywhere he goes.
What is that picture in his back pocket?
Only Mrs. Bemis knows.
At 9 o'clock sharp, she turns the key
Ready to start another day.
Goes into his office, sets his mail on the desk
And before she turns away
She glimpses an ashtray with two cigarettes
Burned down. One has lipstick on the end
There are two wine glasses
One for white one for red
And a letter with a note that says please send.
It's addressed to one of his students.
The envelope is small like a thank you note.
It is stamped and ready but it didn't seal,
And she sneaks a peek at what he wrote.
He's got a picture in his back pocket
Takes it with him everywhere he goes.
What is that picture in his back pocket
Only Mrs. Bemis knows.

Mrs. Bemis knows? What does she know?

So, the amazing Mrs. Bemis is back in the picture. Department secretary extraordinaire. And, if this song is any indication, a bit of a snoop. Someone in the office had a picture that Holly wants Linda to see. And some kind of message on a note.

Linda wondered if Mrs. Bemis will remember anything after all of this time, but she had to try.

When Mrs. Bemis opened the door, Linda's first thought was a reminder of how well she had aged. She was about 10 years older than Linda, but could have been a peer. Her hair was only just starting to fade as gray mixed in very subtly. The lines around her mouth and eyes were small creases and she had not given in to letting herself go. Maybe that came with staying on the job so many years after others might have retired. She wore khaki trousers, sharply creased, and a white oxford collar shirt. Her hair was neatly curled and lipstick and eyeliner meticulously applied. *Take a memo, Linda Harner Metzner - she makes you look like a bag lady.*

Her very appearance encouraged Linda. Someone who looked that great on the outside was likely to have a sharp memory.

"Linda, it is so nice to see you. Come in." Linda was bursting to get right to the task, but knew she should start with the pretense of a social call.

And so, for about an hour, she drank tea and they exchanged the history of their lives, the husbands buried, the career anecdotes. Mrs. Bemis had children and she related each of their stories with vigor in great detail.

Finally, Linda felt that she could bring up Holly McNab.

"Here's something that might interest you. It will be in the paper shortly. They found a body buried in my back field. Turns out it is that of a student who went missing forty years ago. Her name was Holly McNab. That ring any bells?"

Mrs. Bemis frowned with concentration. "Yes, I am remembering something. But I am not quite sure. . ."

Linda reached into her bag and pulled out the copy of Holly's photo.

As Mrs. Bemis held the photo, Linda could see recognition dawning on her face. "Why yes. Yes. I remember this photo. I remember seeing it - in Alex's office. I went in to clean up one night and . . . ."

She stopped. "Oh Linda, I don't think this is proper for me to talk about, even after all these years."

Linda hoped that her beating heart couldn't be discerned through her shirt. "Oh, that's ok, Mrs. Bemis. I know how attractive Alex was to the ladies and that he often acted on that attraction. Before he met me of course."

"Oh oh - yes of course. And it was nothing really. He had a late conference one night. The door was shut and he told me it was ok to leave. So, I did. But I came in very early the next day, as I usually did, and looked around for whatever tidying up needed to be done. When I looked in Alex's office I saw that it was evident he had had a guest, and I thought I would clean up the mess. Then I saw a note."

"A note? From Alex?"

"Yes, . . . oh, Linda I really don't know if I should be telling you this..."

"It's ok, Mrs. Bemis. That was a part of Alex's past that I wasn't part of. What did the note say? And what about this photograph that you recognize?"

"I really shouldn't remember this," she laughed ruefully. "I guess my photographic memory is what made me so good at this job. Well, the picture was signed, 'Thank you for all you have done for me, Holly.' The little note said 'Thanks for the picture. It will go in my wallet with all of my other important things.' No signature though. Just the initials, A.M."

Linda was able to keep her composure as she thanked Mrs. Bemis and said, oh yes of course, let's do it again, and so glad to see you well, and so forth, but as soon as her feet hit the pavement her head exploded, her heart pounded, and her feet made a beeline to the park where she knew she could walk and think.

Alex was involved with Holly? If the song painted a consistent picture, it might have been Holly who was in his office that night, drinking wine and giggling. She wrote a note. From Holly.

Ok. Slow down brain. Stop pounding heart. This doesn't mean anything. You know how all the girls loved Alex, and Holly was a pretty girl. Maybe she flirted with everyone.

But Holly wanted her to know. Why? That Alex was the father of her child? She wasn't good at math, but Linda did a little subtraction. Yes, the time Holly would have gone to Montreal was when Alex was still teaching here. But she never mentions him in her diary. She was in love with a "Mr. B". And her brain started insisting: *He could not have killed her, for Pete's sake, we weren't here when she came back.*

But Linda knew now that this wouldn't be over until she found out the father of Holly's baby. That might even lead to discovering how she had died.

When she had regained her composure, Linda walked home quickly and made a call.

"Jamie? I have another favor to ask."

"What's up?"

"Could you come take a second look at that headstone out back? Would you know how to find out where it might have been made?"

"Ah, fair maiden in distress. My grandfather

was a stonemason actually."

"I should have known. When you have a chance can you look examine it more closely?

"Definitely. I have some time on Thursday. I'll be by about 10?"

"I will look forward to it."

On Thursday, they walked together easily, not speaking. Jamie seemed to sense that this was laying heavy on Linda's mind, and together they allowed the chilled air and the sunshine to do the talking. They came to the river and hiked up onto the promontory.

Jamie knelt and closely examined the stone.

"Could you find out anything without taking it with you?" Linda asked.

"Yeah, I think so." He took a notepad from his pocket and sketched the design. "It looks a little rough, like it was done in a hurry, but I think it is by a pro. You would have to have the right tools to do this. I will take it to some folks I know and see what I can sort out."

He turned a gazed at her reflectively.

"I won't ask why, but for some reason this is important to you."

"Yes," she said quietly. "For some reason it is."

They walked back as quietly as they had come, and the few leaves that were left on the trees shimmered and fluttered as they fell.

"I've always liked this time in the winter,"

he said. "I know that the land is sleeping and getting ready to come back to life at a later time. I feel it is a time when I can rest as well. Work in my shop by the wood stove. I can chisel the angles slowly and sand away the rough of edges with my hand plane for the varnishing yet to come. My creations will come to life in the spring."

Linda gave him a sidewise glance and with a slight upturn of her lips said, "Ok, you did not major in Woodworking and Philosophy. You majored in Poetry."

He laughed hardily. She laughed along, and they reached her door in companionable silence.

He opened the door to his truck and said, "I will see what I can find out Linda. But don't get your hopes up. It was a long time ago."

"I know. But thank you for trying."

Chapter Nineteen

Slipping Into Gothic

Linda was unsure if she would be able to handle the quiet. She had already wondered if she could handle the tension. *I feel like I am caught in some freakin' Daphne DuMaurier novel. Round and round it all goes in my head. It might explode.*

She knew it was time to share this with Maureen. Just an hour later they were at their favorite table at Stella's.

"Maureen, I just don't know what to make of this? I mean, Alex can't possibly be involved in this girl's death! We weren't even here then, and what about Mr. B? Holly never mentions Alex in her diary." Linda swirled the Pinot Noir around and gazes at it as if it has the solution.

Maureen put her hand on her friend's arm. "I'm sure he didn't, Linda. You are right. You guys were gone. But you have to come to terms with the fact that Alex would have been here about the time that Holly went missing."

"I know, I know," she sighed. "But why do I feel like I am living some kind of double life."

"Well," Maureen said quietly, "because Alex was. You have to come to grips with that too. You know, Linda, according to Carrie, Holly was very impressionable. She didn't know her really well, but she seemed to get attached easily to some guy or another. Alex may have been just one in a long line that included Michael Thompson and Mr. Burnette, and perhaps others."

Linda cheered slightly. "Yes, that's true. I remember how it was when I first came here. The line of girls gathered around his door. Alex was only human."

"Yes, and he hadn't married you yet. You changed him. Forever."

Linda told Maureen about her next step. "I figure the only way to put this all to an end is to find out what happened to Holly. I asked Jamie Caldor to see if he can find out who made that gravestone."

"Linda, you are a genius. Yes, it might not

be definitive, but it seems that the only person who could have put that stone there was the one who either killed her or found her body after she fell in and drowned."

"That's what I figure."

"Please let me know when you find out. I guess if anyone can track it down, Jamie can." She gave Linda a hug as she left. "Don't get down. Go do something fun while you wait."

Linda walked down to the ArtHouse Cinema to indulge in an old movie. They always had an old movie playing on Saturday afternoons. She looked at the marquee. *Rebecca*. Joan Fontaine and Lawrence Olivier. *Well, I think I'll pass on that. Give me some good old Abbott and Costello.*

When she got home, she busied herself with gardening and then pulled out a very complicated piano piece. The concentration that comes with years of practice took over temporarily, and she lost herself for a time in Frederic Chopin.

She was roused from her search for the perfect arpeggio when the phone rang.

"Linda, this is Jamie. How are you?"

"Doing fairly well. Will be better if you have any information for me."

"Some. I did find the company that most likely made that stone. A little family-owned granite-carving place on the outskirts of nearby Midlington. I thought I recognized the style. They always specialized in small jobs. However, it would have been old Mr. Razzone who did the work and he has passed on. His son is running the business, but he is almost certain that that is his father's work. He said he will try to find the old paperwork. His dad saved everything, and there are a lot of old records stored in the office attic. All we can do until then is wait I guess."

"Well, I am getting used to that!" she laughed.

"Have you seen today's paper?"

"No, I haven't."

"Well, the young woman's picture is in it, and an article asking for information."

The old foreboding hit Linda's chest. She wanted to know, but she didn't want to know. She wished again that she had never come back to Greenbriar.

Small towns don't change as fast as other places, and it wasn't long before someone called the police office with information.

"Mrs. Metzner?"

"Hello Sheriff."

"A woman has come forward to say that she recognizes the picture in the paper. She said that her parents took in a child brought to them by a woman that she is sure looked like Holly. However, she thinks the woman called herself by some other name and paid them in cash to take care of him. She and her family kept the baby for a few months until the mother came by one day and said that she and the baby's father would be getting married soon."

Married soon. Could Holly have expected she could convince Mr. Burnette to marry her?

Chapter Twenty

Love Letters

I got your letter, Linda said. Do you say that to all the girls? She smiled at him.

The greatest love stories of all time have been written down and communicated through letters you know, he smiled back. A lost art. Now we just get on the telephone. Mystique gone. So, will you? Go to dinner with me tonight?

As she drifted off to sleep, Linda saw his letters.

Perfectly written, his penmanship so unique and flawless, his prose perfect. She sifted though them mentally - so many years past.

Their quick courtship. But she hadn't saved them. Linda, in the foolishness of youth, had not realized their importance once she had married him. She had not seen what they might mean to her in the future.

Dear Linda, love Alex. The letters swirled and danced.

Then a song came through the mix.

Just pieces of paper some might say
Meaning so little and meaning so much.
I'll keep these til my dying day,
As tender as a touch.
Love letters love letters
Telling me that I'm the one one one
Yeah,
Love letters, love letters,
Telling me that I'm the one, one, one.
So many secrets written down
Captive in pen and ink.
The only way to reveal
Things unsaid we feel and think.
Love letters love letters
Telling me that I'm the one one one

Yeah,
Love letters, love letters,
Telling me that I'm the one, one, one.
Foolish girl who does not keep
The talisman from long ago
When love would keep her from her sleep
And words the only way to show
The things he felt, the artful plea
Hidden from all other eyes
Only she can hear and see
What might take others by surprise.
Love letters love letters
Telling me that I'm the one one one
Yeah,
Love letters, love letters,
Telling me that I'm the one, one, one.

Linda woke suddenly. There is something else she is trying to remember. The numbers 111. Telling me that I'm the one, one, one.

The key. She had found it inside of Holly's diary but it had not seemed to belong anywhere. She rose and shook off the sleep and went to her jewelry box. There it was, wrapped in its little velvet envelope.

The light filtering in indicated that the day was well underway, and a glance at the clock confirmed it. She splashed water on her face and shook her head hard. She wasn't sure where to go with this, but she felt an urgency to go somewhere with it.

She threw on jeans and a turtleneck and heavy jacket, as the weather was harsh, and headed to the only place she could think of - the locksmith on Main. Perhaps he could help identify this key. It wasn't a house or a car key, nor was it small enough for a locker. It had a peculiar imprint that might help identify it. She didn't yet know why this would help, but she just knew she had to try.

A small chime sounded as she opened up the store to Harrison's Lockshop. "Good morning," the man behind the desk said cheerfully. "What can I do you for?'

"Good morning to you as well! I am Linda Metzner. I just moved into Greenbriar and I found a strange key behind some old boxes in the garage and thought it would be interesting to track it down."

"Super! I love this kind of stuff. I am assuming you have it with you?"

"Of course!" She laughed. She reached in her pocketbook and drew out the small velvet pouch. She slipped the small brass key from the pouch and handed it to him.

He didn't have to examine it long. "This is a post office box key. Greenbriar Post Office used keys just like this until 1970 I think, when we re-did the entire PO and replaced them with different locks. Very cool. But I am afraid it doesn't really have any value, and it is likely that the box it opened is long gone. But, you know, if you really are on a treasure hunt, go down to the antique store - Miller's - right in the center of town. Hattie Miller used to be Post Mistress around that time. She might be able to give you more information."

"Why, yes. I have been there. Bought a settee from her. I do remember her telling me that she had been Post Mistress. I guess if anyone has more information about this key, it would be Hattie. Thank you." She smiled. "Do you charge for advice?"

"Not a cent. Just remember me when you want to change the locks on your house."

"I certainly will."

The wind almost blew Linda back against the door. *This better be worth it. I could be at home in front of my fire.* But she knew that all that would yield would be restlessness. Better to keep charging along, no matter how uncomfortable it was.

"Mrs. Metzner! Lovely to see you again. I hope that you aren't dissatisfied with your settee?"

"Not at all. I love it. It fits perfectly into the space intended and Jamie Caldor has proved to be a very handy man to know."

"Yes, Jamie is a master of all trades. Smart too. I remember he graduated at the top of his class. Always thought he'd finish college the same way, but I think he was smart enough to know that he loved to work with his hands and that his family business was worth keeping going. So is it more furniture you're needing?"

"I am not surprised at any of that. No, no more furniture just yet. I am on the hunt for information. Hoping to kill a few cats with my curiosity."

She pulled out the key and handed it to Mrs. Miller.

"My goodness! Where did you get this? It's an old Post Office box key from our previous facility here in Greenbriar."

"How can you be sure?"

"We had a distinctive set up. Our boxes were very old. In fact, we were the last PO in the state to update to a new system."

She read the number aloud. "111. I hate to admit my acquisitive nature, but I couldn't keep from it. When the boxes were torn out, I helped myself to an entire block of them and had some staff bring them over to my storage building. After that, I am afraid I just forgot about them. But something makes me feel that this box, 111, is one of them."

"Well," Linda said, "I don't suppose it matters. They must be empty. But, even so, it might be fun to get hold of this one. Perhaps one of the owners of my house had this box at one time. Maybe I could buy it from you? Put it in my sunroom or something."

Hattie blushed a bit. "To be truthful, I nicked

this block of boxes before the USPS could come and take off the doors. They are all pretty intact. I suppose there is a chance that something could still be inside one of them."

Just then, a customer came in. Hattie looked at Linda and pointed to the back. "Through those doors and to your left. Storage unit marked 'C'. Help yourself."

Linda's stomach muscles contracted as she headed in the direction that Hattie indicated. The heavy door opened slowly and she looked around until she found a light connected to a pull chain.

The room was packed to capacity with a variety of items, but it was easy to see the block of post office boxes set against the back wall.

She scanned the numbers on the boxes. Sure enough. There, fairly prominent near the end of the 100 row, was a box with the number 111.

Her hand shook so much she wasn't sure that she could get the key into the lock. It took a little time to maneuver the key until it slipped completely in, but finally it clicked and turned.

The little door swung open. Her heart almost stopped. There was something in the box - a small stack of paper.

Linda left the storage room and headed toward the front showroom toward the outside door.

"Well" said Hattie cheerful. "Find anything? A map to a lost gold mine?"

Linda laughed in what she hoped was a natural manner. "No, totally empty. And I didn't realize that the boxes would be attached to each other so securely. It would be pretty difficult to remove just one."

"That's true. But you have me thinking. I should probably put that whole block up for sale. Somebody's bound to want it. Thanks for reminding me about them. Maybe you could frame the key in a shadow box or something? If you want some other trinkets of that era, let me know."

"Great idea. I certainly will."

Linda made up some excuse for why she had to hurry away and, as the large door blew closed behind her, she clutched her bag close to her chest.

Well, Alex, I am now not just a liar, I am a thief.

When she got home, she spread them out on her table. Seven folded pieces of paper, but they had no envelopes.

They had been opened, and Linda guessed that Holly chose to store them in the box. To keep them from being found perhaps? After she opened them did Holly used the box to store them safely, away from prying eyes? There were no dated stamped envelopes, however numbers had been written on the outside of each of letter. The order in which they had been received?

1: Dear Holly Doll,

I got your message that you want to meet me at our special place. I can make it tomorrow at 10 pm.

I have written you a new poem:

> I hear her laugh.
> It floats through the night breeze and
> Lights the night sky with
> A ripple of sweetness.
> I see her smile.
> It shimmers through the clouds
> And is a sweet spray of summer,
> Rain on the parched ground.
> I smell her hair.
> Hints of lavender and lemon
> Caress my fingers
> And coat them with the
> Promise of tomorrow's touches.
> She is the fresh fruit of all of my senses.
> Dangling so near and yet so far.
> Soon I will walk through the garden of our love
> And place her in the basket of my life.
> Hope you like it.

Mr. B

2:

Holly, I have been thinking about your news. Are you sure it is mine? I know you having been dating a few men. To go through with this would not be in your best interests. You need to finish school. I think I can help you. I will talk to some people and get back to you.

3:

I have taken the liberty to contact Sylvie Blake. She can help you. You can find her at 23 Campus Drive. I contacted her incognito and hope that you will understand why my name can't come into this.

4:

Holly, I understand why this will be hard for you, but Dr. Morgentaler is very competent. You would be in the best hands. You will be able to have another child in time, I am sure, when you are ready for a child and can be a good mother to it. You are much too young right now. You have no idea what taking care of a child entails. And you know I can't help you. Good luck.

5:

Holly, I am so surprised to hear from you and very disappointed to find that you did not visit the clinic. I supposed you had gone home. I am leaving Greenbriar as well. Please don't contact me again.

6:

I received your request for money and I will send some, but there is only so much I can do. Yes, you are capable of ruining my life, as you say. But, I have tried to help you as much as I can. I can't marry you, as you demand. I am not even sure this child is mine. Maybe you aren't even sure. No one would believe you anyway and your life would be ruined. Please, let this be. Leave Greenbriar. Go home to your family. I am sure that they will understand.

7:

Holly, your last letter was very disconcerting. You can't possibly be going to go through with this. You claim that you have proof that will reveal everything. I can't see how that could be. I am coming to see you. We just need to sit down and discuss this. I will meet you at our old spot next week, Thursday, at 10 pm. All will be well.

Linda re-folded and stacked the letters and leaned back in her chair. She closed her eyes and sighed deeply as the long shadows crept under the eaves.

Closer, but still so far.

Chapter Twenty-One

Written In Stone

As usual, the light of day didn't make things any more clear to Linda after a restless sleep. *Come on girl. This has to end. You have to start asking the tough questions.*

She called Maureen. "Would Carrie be willing to talk to me about Holly?"

"Oh, I am sure she would. But she didn't seem to know very much."

"Well, maybe I can ask her some direct questions that will help her remember some things."

Linda walked up to the door, and hesitated

just slightly before knocking. Another deep breath.

Carrie was a small, cherubic woman given to weight gain, totally gray, but with a charismatic smile that made her seem 18 years old.

"Hello Mrs.Metzner! It has been a long time!"

"You remember me?" Linda was surprised.

"Sure. I never had a class with you, but you were on some panels I attended. I always admired your presentation skills."

"Well, that is gratifying to know. So sorry to be abrupt and to bother you about things that happened so long ago, but your sister tells me that you knew the young girl that we have found buried in my back yard. Holly McNab?"

"Yes. So sad. Are the police any closer to finding out about her? I hear she was buried with a child?"

"Seems so, yes. No, they haven't found out much. I guess I feel some obligation to help with the research because she was found on my property, but I didn't know her personally. I thought maybe if we chatted about random memories, something might reveal itself that you hadn't thought of before."

"Of course! When we unlock our minds, things come out that we least expect."

She thought a moment and then said, "All of us have wonders hidden in our breasts, only needing circumstances to evoke them."

Linda laughed. "Charles Dickens. So you were paying attention in someone's English Class."

Carrie looked pleased. "Yes. Your husband's in fact. Freshman year I was in his Introductory Lit class."

This seemed like an opportune moment to segue. "Oh really? You had a class with Alex? Was Holly in that class too?"

"Why yes, she was in fact. I had forgotten that."

"Did Holly like it? Was English her major?"

No, I think she was undeclared, but leaning toward Psychology. Probably took it as an elective. Humanities requirement."

"Ah yes. Did you like Alex as a teacher?"

"Oh yes. Dr. Metzner was very personable. Everyone loved his class."

"Holly too?"

"We never talked too much about it, but let me think. Something is getting stirred in my head with all of the current events. Yes, Holly seemed to like Alex a lot. She thought he was very handsome. One day she said to me as we left class. 'Isn't he dreamy? I think I will call him Mr. Beautiful.' "

The sky turned to steel and then a vise wrapped around Linda's throat as this sunk in. *Mr. Beautiful. Monsieur B.? Could it be*?

"Mrs. Metzner are you ok? Would you like some water?"

Linda nodded soundlessly and by the time

Carrie returned with a glass of water, she had regained her composure.

Linda drank the water and then excused herself.

"Thanks Carrie. I guess we didn't accomplish much, but it was very nice to hear your reminisces."

"If I think of anything else, I will give you a call."

"That would be wonderful."

Linda walked home in a frozen stupor, hardly noticing anything or anyone around her. She fumbled with her key, let herself into her house and collapsed on the sofa.

Well you wanted to know. You wanted to ask the tough questions. Slow down. Free your mind. All of us have wonders hidden in our breasts.

Mr. B. But we were gone. She bolted up quickly and unwrapped the letters again and spread them out of the table. "Request for money." "Meet you at our old spot."

Perhaps it was a coincidence but perhaps not. Just then, her eyes lit on a favorite statuette on her mantel. The ancient Greek Goddess of Memory, Mnemosyne. She was always portrayed with serene elegance. Her presence was powerful, filled with a meditative quality. Ever since childhood, Linda had loved the Ancient Greek myths. Not knowing how to explain the unexplainable, the Greeks had created the gods and goddesses.

Mnemosyne, she remembered, was one of the

most powerful because she was the emblem of the human consciousness, the special gift that distinguishes man from other animals, that ability to reason and to remember that is the very foundation of civilization.

Remember, Linda. Try to remember. She filled her diffuser with a combination of mint and lavender and lay down. Deep breaths, slow rhythmic pulls on her consciousness.

I have to leave for a few days Linda. I have been offered a speaking gig at New York University.

Oh wonderful! When? Maybe I can get the time off?

It is rather sudden. Next week. I will be gone Thursday and Friday. Really, it wouldn't be much fun for you and at this point in your career to be absent much is not a good thing. I won't be away long.

His face disappeared and she saw a ledger. Long columns of figures. She had her checkbook out and was perplexed.

Alex, I can't get this to balance. In fact, some checks are missing. We seem to have less money in our account than I can account for.

Oh, probably those last charitable contributions

I made. I know we usually do those together, but an alum from Yale called begging, and I couldn't say no. Don't worry about it. You have better things to angst over.

A cloud rose and bathed in her scent, and the vision of Mnemosyne shattered and disappeared along with her dream. Linda awoke from her reverie with a start.

The tough questions. *What was that famous line from <u>She Stoops To Conquer</u>? "Ask me no questions, I'll tell you no fibs."*

Right now she could use a dose of fibs. The pit in her stomach widened and sunk like a lead weight.

Linda spent the rest of the day rolling all the possibilities around in her head. There was still a whole bunch of circumstantial stuff going on here. Certainly not enough evidence to prove that Alex fathered Holly's child, paid her hush money, and then when she threatened to expose their relationship, came back and killed her and the child.

Why? Why would he feel he had to do that? He would know that she would have dealt with it and would have supported him in trying to help this girl.

She suddenly heard some music. A snippet. It sounded familiar. *Yes Holly? What is it?*

Words she has heard before come through the air as if to remind her of something.

And words the only way to show
The things he felt, the artful plea
Hidden from all other eyes.
Only she can hear and see
What might take others by surprise.

"Hidden from all other eyes? Might take others by surprise?"

Perhaps the key here is that Holly didn't have any secrets that would hurt Alex, but maybe she knew things that would hurt Larry Martin? Things that would destroy him and the deception he had work so hard to create? Something he couldn't even tell his wife?

Just when it was all becoming too much to bear, the doorbell rang.

A young man she did not know greeted her. "Mrs. Metzner? Linda Metzner?"

"Yes?"

"My name is Anthony Razzone. Jamie Caldor was asking if we had any information about a carved stone in your backyard. Well, my dad was able to find the old bill of sale in my Grandfather's records. Sorry, it doesn't have any name attached to it."

He handed the sketch and the bill to her. "Hope it means something to you." He nodded at her and got back into his car.

The drawing matched the engraving that was on the stone. There was no name, just writing:

From that professor fella who used to teach at the college. Hurry job."

Linda quietly closed the door. She turned and, for a moment, just stared blankly at the carved mantelpiece that was the focal point of the living room. *Alex loved that mantel.*

Then she threw herself upon the sofa and sobbed.

Chapter Twenty-Two

Ashes to Ashes

Linda dreamed. Fragments melded together, bits and pieces of faces, words, places, bound in light and darkness. She said yes upon a grassy promontory and looked deeply into the water. There is nothing for me here, he said, and drove away around the dangerous curve. She followed to a small graveyard in a little town in Washington and laid flowers on a grave. The grave morphed into a hole next to a small, engraved stone. Mother and Child. She walked the Greenbriar College hallways and gazed wistfully at young Alex in all his beauty. He looked at her and smiled. I'm really Larry you know, he said. He took her to his office and pointed proudly at his diplomas. Yale. He opened a door and inside were his books. I wrote these books he said proudly. You see, he looked at her intently. I could do it. I wasn't a nothing. He would have been so proud. So proud. So proud. His voice faded and Linda was alone again, turning the key. It wasn't the same key. It wasn't the same lock. Then the flower girl sang. You think you have the key. You always thought you were the one who knew him best. Silver Coins have two sides. Secrets in pen and ink. Please give me a name, a name, a name.

Music. She heard a refrain floating through the air. She saw a vision, a misty face, a light. The melody was familiar but these were new words:

Take a look in the chest up there in the attic
For things that he kept out of sight
There are things he will tell you
He wants you to know
Someday when the time is right

Things he wants me to know when the time is right. The chest. Linda hurriedly dressed and didn't even bother with coffee.

The chest was where it had been when she last looked and she opened it again, this time paying very close attention to everything. She took out the entire contents, examining each carefully before laying it on the floor beside her. There was nothing she hadn't seen before. She reached in and lightly stroked the sides of the lining of the wooden box. Just as she was about to give up, she felt a portion of the velvet top compress slightly. She flipped the box on its side and using her fingers felt around until she found a place where the fabric gave way. She slowly pushed the lining aside and saw something taped to the top of the chest. An envelope.

She gently opened the envelope and saw what appeared to be a letter inside. She unfolded it and read the first sentence.

Dear Linda. If you are reading this, then I am most likely dead. It is best if you don't find it, because that means you are happily living out your life. However, if you do find it, perhaps it is because you have gone looking for answers. I want you to know these answers.

Linda folded the letter, put it back in the envelope and, without putting anything back in the chest, walked down the stairs to coffee and the light. She was sure she would need it. It had become standard procedure.

"This won't be long. It isn't necessary that I relate

to you the entire story of my life like some sort of latter-day Nicholas Nickleby. However, you might be surprised to find that there are certain Dickensian elements to my journey, some of which I feel only fair that you should know.

First, above all, I want to assure you that you have been the love of my life. You redeemed me and gave me that sense of acceptance and unconditional love I always longed for. You took my elusive and scattered parts and knit them into a being whose existence seemed justified on this planet. Nothing that happened in my life before or after you mattered. However, there are things inside of us that we cannot shed easily, fears that we embody, things that even those we love and who love us best could not easily comprehend and forgive.

I don't know what led you to this letter. Chance perhaps. Or perhaps events transpired that caused you to go searching for more of me. Perhaps you became curious about things that had never, in your sweet, accepting nature, crossed your mind.

I will keep this brief. There are really only a few things you need to know. First of all, my birth name is not Alex Metzner. I was born Larry Martin, in Ridgefield, Washington to small town privilege and expectations that I somehow could not manage to live up to. When my best friend, an orphan named

Alex Metzner, had a tragic accident, I seized the opportunity to steal his identity and spirit myself away without anyone knowing.

I was hungry, Linda, hungry for all that Alex was and I was not: an athlete, a scholar, and a kind, giving, unpretentious soul who was given so little and yet achieved so much. I envied the pride he elicited from my father who saw in Alex so much of what he did not see in me.

And so, when fate conspired in a manner so twisted as to rival the best of Shakespeare's tragedies, I let it carry me. It carried me to those places Alex was meant to go and I was meant to miss. His transcripts got me into Yale and my determination to be like him, to think like him, to achieve like him, carried me the rest of the way.

I don't like having to remember that day, but I know you will be wondering. One night Alex, being the more mature of the two of us, insisted on returning home after a long jaunt to the country. I didn't want to leave to go home. I had found a girl I wanted to know better. But Alex knew that my family would be very upset if we didn't come back that night, so he took my new car, one he wasn't really trained to drive, and took a bad turn around a mountain. To avoid a truck, he rammed right into a tree. He was burned beyond recognition.

When my newest girlfriend brought me home, I heard about the accident on the radio. I don't know what possessed me, but immediately I thought, "Run for it. This is your fault and you will be blamed." I already had Alex's belongings that he had left behind in the cabin, including a nice wad of cash he had saved up. I hid nearby in a small motel, and when I realized that everyone thought the body was mine, it just seemed the natural thing to do. The girl I was with thought I was Alex too. She headed back where she had come from without knowing differently.

Coincidentally, Alex and I had decided to switch identities that night, just for fun. We put on each other's clothes, right down to my uncle's dog tags. There was no one who knew that I was Larry Martin and that Alex Metzner was burnt to ash that night.

And so, like some modern-day Jekyll and Hyde, I have carried with me two personalities, always torn between who I was and who I wanted to be.

When you came along, I thought, at last! Now I am whole. I have become the person of distinction I have always craved. I have found my soul mate – the kind of woman that Alex would have married and Dad would have approved of. My sense of self-respect expanded. I almost fooled myself. However, we carry our pasts with us. I almost escaped mine, but it was not to be. A young student became infatuated with me and foolishly, though briefly, I thought I was in love.

.

I wrote her love letters, and I gave in to her seduction. She showed up at my office one day and she said that I fathered her child. This was all before I met you, Linda, believe that. Had I met you first, this never would have happened.

I did my best to help her. I arranged for her to have a safe abortion and helped her to be accepted to another school out West. I thought it was over. I know you were surprised by my sudden decision to leave Greenbriar, but I had actually been planning it for a while. I wanted a clean slate. I wanted to be a different man.

But she had other plans. She did not have the abortion. Just before you and I left Greenbriar, she contacted me. I began to get letters from her at my office. I thought it would end after we left, but she began blackmailing me and sending me notes to my office in PA. She first asked for money, to assure her promise that she would never reveal our liaison and child. I gave her some money, but then realized there would be no end to that. And so, I decided I would tell you the entire story. Perhaps, I thought, we could adopt the child.

When I suggested that to her, she changed. She no longer wanted my money; she wanted me to divorce you and marry her. If I did not, she would reveal to the world the entire story of my false identity that I had so stupidly confessed to her after one too many drinks and ego-fueled caresses.

And so, my dearest Linda, Mr. Hyde came out of the shadows. I made an excuse to be gone for a few days and went back to Greenbriar to talk with her. Feigning affection for her, I lured her into meeting me down by the river behind our house.

I didn't have any real intentions at the time. I just wanted to make sure she realized she would have to drop her scheme. To my surprise, she showed up with the child. Linda, he did not look like me, I swear. I felt no affinity with this child, but I meant him no harm.

"I named him after you," she said." I named him Larry." I am not proud of how I treated her. But she smiled with a smile so fixed and stubborn it set something off inside of me. "He is not my child," I yelled, and swore she wouldn't get away with it.

"I wrote it all down," she said. "I wrote your real name and all about the accident. All anyone has to do is take your picture to your friends and family

and they will verify who you really are. I will say you killed Alex to take his identity. I will say you were driving and you left him to die. All you have worked for will be ruined. Your little Linda will find you hideous and appalling. Leave her, marry me, take care of your child."

I reached for her and told her I would take the child and care for it but that she and I had no future. Without a child, I told her, she could reinvent herself. She could get on with her life. But her grasp on the child was stronger than I knew, and they both tumbled into the stream that was running high and fast. I followed them downstream, but when I fished them out, they were both dead.

I didn't know what to do, so I carried them up to the promontory where I knew they would remain dry. I hid them behind some bushes and drove to a hardware store for a tarp and some quicklime and I buried them. Later I had a stone made for them.

You will find it where I courted you - where I said I wanted to be buried someday. As I write this, I am disgusted with myself, but I think in a way I was burying them with some kind of honor. By leaving them on that high, dry cliff that meant so much to me, I might somehow atone for my sins through this modest and insufficient expiation.

I don't think there is much left to tell. This great lie of my life led to more lies and to great act of cruelty.

My purgatory has been the knowledge that I may have killed my only son, something I was somehow able to block, just as I had blocked the reality that I was not actually Alex Metzner but rather Larry Martin. I made my own reality sometimes. Perhaps I thought that by becoming Alex I could somehow pay him back for my selfish choice that cost him his life.

Sweet, sweet Linda. I wish we had conceived a child together so that he could take the best of me with him through this world under the tempering influence of your beautiful character.

If you read this letter, I hope that you will forgive me and know that I wish for you a long, happy life with someone who is a much better person than I was.

Love,
Alex (Larry)

Linda folded the letter gently and put it back in its envelope. As she wiped away tears, she was somehow relieved to have this confirmation of what she had learned, and so glad she hadn't just stumbled on this letter out of the blue. So Alex had not killed Larry intentionally to get his identity – it had been an accident, as had Holly's death as well. She sensed sincerity in this letter - Alex had no way of knowing when he wrote it that she might find out his secrets someday. There was a great deal more atonement than apology in this letter. It was an attempt to seek forgiveness.

She remembered Alex's description of the encounter. The description that the coroner gave of the damage to the bones that mother and child incurred would seem to match the deaths in his narrative.

She reached into the hidden drawer in her desk and extracted her copy of Holly's diary. But a thorough re-reading yielded very little. That Holly had tended toward over-the-top infatuation for several men, not just Alex, was evident, but the entire tone of the writing was more girlish than it as devious or conniving. Would she really have lied to Alex? Certainly motherhood must change a person. The girl who did not go to Montreal came back to Greenbriar a mother who would do anything for her child.

Linda thought back to that era when she had come of age, when girls had fewer choices.

"Given a different set of circumstances," she thought, "I might have been Holly."

She sensed Holly's presence in the room and turned to see her there. She looked almost real.

"Good for you Holly." Linda whispered. She

was suddenly ashamed that she had judged the girl like everyone else had. "Good for you for trying to be strong, to ask for what you deserved. I apologize for thinking you were a giddy girl who slept around. You simply loved a man, a man who didn't want to live up to his responsibilities. It was a very strong thing you did, to bring the child back to Greenbriar. But in today's world, you could have been stronger. You could have said good riddance to a man who didn't want you; you could have gone back to your home and raised this child. It wouldn't have meant today what it meant then. You might have lived."

The girl's light glowed for a moment, and Linda thought she saw the hint of a smile as the flower girl faded slowly away.

So much became clear now. It wasn't his relationship with Holly that Alex needed to hide. He wasn't afraid of a love child. And it wasn't his academic reputation that he was protecting, either. It was his self-esteem.

Holly had known who he really was. All his charade, those achievements that he had sacrificed so much for, would be revealed. His personal vindication of youthful dismissal from his father, all gone. How could he have stood being unmasked? How could he have recovered from the loss of his esteem and the regard he had been given? It would have meant nothing for him to have proved to his family and friends that he had been able to succeed. They would only see the lies. They might have believed him capable of killing for it. It would have destroyed him.

There in her desk, next to scanned diary pages, was a small propane lighter. She flicked the wheel with her thumb and touched the flame to a corner of the letter and, as it crumbled into ashes, she thought Alex truly wasn't sure that the child was his. He had made a last attempt to save it. He wanted her to know that. And something from the very first song came floating back to her.

When a song comes out of nowhere
It will haunt you like a ghost
And it will make you question
The things you love the most.
It will set on fire
Much that you hold dear
When a song comes out of nowhere.

Sometimes it is best to burn the past.

Chapter Twenty-Three

Mrs. McNab

Linda knew she had to verify the identity of the baby's father; it was very important somehow. Alex had not admitted to being the father, and it had to be very clear. She needed to know. Holly had sung *"Please give me a name"*. Maybe that applies to the little child as well. If the baby were Alex's, Holly had wanted to give him his name.

For several days, Linda was happy to bide her time holed up in her house, reading, cleaning, organizing, doing anything to keep her mind occupied as she awaited the DNA results.

Sheriff Wallace had helped her arrange for Alex's body to be exhumed and for DNA to be extracted from his teeth and bones.

She had swallowed hard when she went into his office to explain. She told him Carrie's story about how Holly had called Alex "Mr. Beautiful". "I'm sure you remember from the diary that Holly was infatuated with a Mr. B. And we have Mrs. Bemis' memory of Holly having visited Alex in his office and his note to her. I don't know anything for sure, Sheriff. It seems like a tenuous link, but this is something I need to know."

She hadn't told the sheriff about her research on the stone, nor shared with anyone, even Jamie, what the receipt had said. If it somehow got revealed, by young Anthony Razzone perhaps, it is still a very flimsy link to murder. Heck, she didn't even remember his going back to buy the stone.

She paused. "I hope that this isn't something that needs to go public. And even if Alex is the father, it wouldn't mean that he had killed her." She didn't share that she had found the letter. *No one else needs ever to know about that.*

He looked at her softly. "No, it doesn't. I can't promise anything, though. I have to do my job." She nodded.

She drove the six hours to Philadelphia for the exhumation, thankful that the soil was soft enough for it on a winter's day. She knelt down at the tombstone and traced the name, just as she had traced the name of Larry Martin. Alexander James Metzner. Born August 1, 1936. Died March 12, 2011. *I am sorry Alex. This has to be done.*

She didn't watch the exhumation, but instead just returned to Greenbriar, thinking all the way, and waited.

When she received the sample from the lab in Pennsylvania, she took it down to the coroner's office that had done the testing on Holly and the child.

The coroner called with the results. "Mrs. Metzner? I have the results of the test. It does appear that the bones of the child share mitochondrial DNA with the sample you gave us. I have to pass this information on to the Sheriff's office. He may be calling you."

Linda felt as if a weight had fallen off of her shoulders. Once again, she had to admit that there is something in discovering the definite that is always satisfying, no matter how hard it is to believe.

"Thank you." She said softly and hung up.

Shortly afterward, she did get a call from the Sheriff.

"Hello, Mrs. Metzner. Got the information back. I am putting this information in my report." There was a slight pause. "I am also writing that this information is not linked in any way to Holly's death. I have decided to not go public with it for that reason. There is no justification for giving this information to the press. I think my job has been to find out the identity of a missing person, and we have done that, thanks to you. However, if any other corroborating evidence appears that links your husband to Holly's death, I will have to pursue it. Otherwise, we are considering this an accidental death by fall or drowning. Who put that stone there, and why, well, I guess that will just remain a mystery."

"I understand, Sheriff. Thank you." She paused. "Sheriff, I hope it is all right if I go see Holly's mother. I just want to take her the diary I found in the house, if I could have it back. I don't think I will tell her about Alex, but if I can bring her comfort in any way, I would like to do that."

"That's ok by me. We don't need the diary any longer. If you have any further needs, just let me know."

"Thanks Sheriff. I really appreciate your kindness."

The next day, Linda made her airline reservations to fly to Montana. Several days later, a taxi dropped her off at an assisted living facility where she was met by a stocky man with a soft voice.

"Mrs. Metzner? I'm Ben McNab. Holly's brother. My mother is very excited to see you. Please, let me take you to her."

Mrs. Ellie McNab was very frail, but her bright eyes indicated that she was totally in command of her mental faculties.

Linda held her withered hand and thanked

her for taking time to see her.

"Why thank you, Mrs. Metzner. I understand that it is because of you that Holly was found and identified. I just wish there was more you might tell me about our dear girl whom we have mourned for so many years. But at least she has come home."

Linda looked at Ben McNab and said, "Ben, would you mind if I had just a little time with your mom alone."

He looked uncertain but when he glanced at his mother, she nodded, and he nodded back and turned to leave. "Maybe not more than 30 minutes? She needs a lot of rest."

"Definitely," she said.

"Mrs. McNab," Linda began.

"Oh please call me Ellie. What is your name?"

"Thank you. You must call me Linda." Ellie smiled and just waited as if she knew something important was about to be said.

"Mrs. M... Ellie.... how do you feel about the possibility that people's spirits live on after them, especially if they have things left unresolved on this earth?

Her bright eyes lit up. "Oh, I believe that strongly! Have you come to say that you have been contacted by my Holly? For so long I had a difficult time believing she was gone because her spirit force was so strong."

Linda sighed. *This is going to be easier than*

I thought.

"Ellie, I believe that Holly's spirit has been in my house. She was singing to me when I arrived, giving me clues as to how to find out about her." Linda omitted the clues that Holly had given that led her to Alex's secret. That was a different secret - one that had to be kept.

Ellie sat up and leaned forward. "Oh my! Tell me more Linda. Did she have a message for me?" Linda reached for her phone and found the song. Holly's mother listened to *The Rain Has Stopped* transfixed, tears slowly building up in her eyes.

"Oh that is Holly!" She exclaimed. "She had such a beautiful voice. What a plaintive message. *Give me a name, tell my momma.* Oh my!" The tears were rolling down her cheeks.

She reached for Linda's hand. "And you have done it Linda. It doesn't matter, any of the rest of it. She is named and she has come home."

"Ellie, they told you that Holly was found with a child?"

She looked very sad. "Yes, and I blame myself for her not coming home. I am a devout Catholic and I believe she would have felt she had been a disappointment to me. What was that line about telling me that she had not veered from what she was taught? What do you suppose that means? She bore a child out of wedlock which was against what she was taught."

"Ellie, I talked to some people who knew Holly, and they indicated that she had been encouraged to go to Canada to get an abortion. She didn't get that abortion Ellie. I think that is what she wants you to know. In some ways it would have been easier for her to do that, but she did what she had been taught and kept the child. That is what she wanted you to know."

"Yes, yes, of course. Life begins at conception is what I believe, and Holly knew that." Then she said sadly. "Dear Holly. I just wish she would have come home. I would have accepted the child and I would have helped her."

She cried.

"I think a girl at that age is very impressionable and certainly her love for you and desire for your approval was so important. I think she was hoping to marry the baby's father before she came home. That didn't work out." Linda spoke quietly and with a gentle assurance that she hoped would be of solace to Ellie.

"Yes, of course. Well, Linda, thank you, thank you. You have brought a bit of my Holly home. We will give her a name. But what about the child? Does it have a name?"

"It's a boy, Ellie. One night Holly whispered to me after she finished singing that his name is Larry. Lawrence Alexander."

Another lie and another assumption, but one that seemed plausible and fitting.

"Lawrence Alexander. That's a nice name. We will put it on the stone."

Linda reached into her purse and handed Mrs. McNab the diary. "There isn't too much in here that helps identify the father or says too much about Holly's college years, but you might want it."

She reached for the diary with trembling white hands, skin so transparent that her purple veins seemed to reside on the outside.

"Oh my. Yes. No matter what, this is her writing, these are her thoughts."

She looked up. "Can I tell Ben? About Holly's ghost?"

"If you think he will understand, it is fine with me."

"Oh, he will. Ben is very much a believer in the forces of the spirit."

Linda leaned over and gave Ellie McNab a kiss on the cheek and said goodbye. As she was waiting for her taxi, she heard a voice behind her.

"Mrs. Metzner!" It was Ben McNab. "My mother just told me." He reached for her hand and said, "Thank you so much. Is it true? Or did you just say those things to help an old woman with her grief."

"No, it's true."

"But Holly said nothing that helps you with how she died?" He looked troubled. "I mean, if it were a suicide, that would destroy Mom."

Linda somehow managed to keep the feeling

from her face. "No, Ben, they suspect some sort of accident was involved. She was buried, remember? Some kind soul buried her and put up a stone. No, they are treating this as an accidental death. They believe she and the child fell into the river and drowned."

She looked at him tenderly. "Certainly if Holly had the strength to bear this child, she would never have taken their lives."

He looked relieved. "Yes, that's right. Holly was always a feisty little thing. There wasn't a suicidal bone in her body. I know that is why she had the conviction to keep the child. Can I hug you?"

She smiled. "Of course."

The power of touch. She had felt it in Ellie McNab's hand and she felt it again in Ben McNab's strong, thankful embrace. Resolution. Completion.

Forgiveness - for Alex and for Holly.

As different as you were, Alex and Holly, you had in common a need to be what your parents wanted you to be. How difficult parenting must be. In planting the seeds that we hope will help our children grow and succeed, it is possible to also set the stage for what might destroy them. Nature vs. Nurture, an age-old conundrum I have not had to face and therefore cannot judge.

Chapter Twenty-Four

New Again

Linda leaned against the side of the plane and attempted to sleep, but instead she stared into the dark clouds. This was her second cross-country trip in the last six months - six months filled with ghosts and graveyards that spanned 60 years and a continent. So much had happened since she had first turned that key in the lock.

For once, she was grateful for the long trip from Boston to Greenbriar. When she boarded the Greyhound bus, she flicked on the overhead light and opened the book she had brought in her carryon bag, but her mind couldn't focus. She found herself going over the recent events in wonder.

Well, it was over now. Holly has a name and Alex has appeased his guilt.

She reached her home and, just as night fell, inserted the key into the lock. It was the same key, it was the same lock, but she felt like she was walking into her house for the first time. She switched on the lights and silently surveyed the interior landscape. "Do you want to stay, Linda," she whispered aloud. Things hadn't turned out in a way that might have been expected. She hadn't planned on a whirlwind of music, research and traveling. Wouldn't she be happier someplace else, someplace away from the memories?

But interestingly, she did not feel sad, afraid, or at all troubled as she lit a fire and made a cup of homecoming tea. It did feel like home. The long trip had left her weary and, as her eyes got heavy, she felt a presence. She opened them and saw a willowy, misty vision. She had thought she wouldn't see it again. She smiled. *Hello Holly. Have you come to say goodbye?*

Holly was sitting in the corner holding her guitar and she began to sing:

You've found the key, unlocked the past
What came first is now the last.

It no longer seems like I have never been,
Thank you for making me feel like I am new again.
The choices of my tender age
Rested heavy in my mind
Although my body left,
My spirit stayed behind
And whispered through the hills
Until it grew old and thin.
Thank you for making me feel
Like I am new again.
Those who live in memory can
leave this world in peace.
I thought my chance to do that was gone.
But now I know that I can just move on.
You opened doors and read my heart
You finished what I couldn't start,
Erased all my mistakes, buried all the sin
Thank you for making me feel like I am new again.
Thank you, thank you.
Because of you I am new again.

Linda didn't bother to record the song this time.

"You are welcome," she whispered and she watched Holly fade away. *We are both new again.*

A calm come over her and Linda knew that it was finally over. Her normal life could resume.

She loved the old house, not because of what it had been, but because it was now home. Her home. Her friends. Her town.

As had been for some time now, the hot shower was welcomed as it washed away the stress of a long travel day. She reached into her drawer and pushed aside the flannel. It made her feel old. She pushed aside the silk. That belonged to Alex. She pulled out a nightdress she had never worn. Long, deep amethyst, and made of Tencel. It flowed smoothly and sensuously around her body and brushed her ankles gently.

She undid her long braid and combed through her hair. She had worn it long for Alex. Tomorrow she would make an appointment to have it cut. Yes. A new beginning. She felt a sense of peace and security. What we know can't hurt us, and she expected no more visitors as she held the good memories of Alex and the good things in their past to her heart.

As she was about to slip between the covers, she realized that the message light on her telephone was flashing.

"You have one message," the dispassionate voice told her.

"Linda? This is Jamie. Hey, I saw your car back in your driveway. Hope your trip went well. Would love to hear about it. When you feel settled in, give me a call if you are in the mood for a little Guinness stew."

Linda hung up and smiled. *Yes. A little Guinness Stew would hit the spot.*

Music, When Soft Voices Die

Music, when soft voices die,
Vibrates in the memory -
Odours, when sweet violets sicken,
Live within the sense they quicken.
Rose leaves, when the rose is dead,
Are heaped for the beloved's bed;
And so thy thoughts,
when thou art gone,
Love itself shall slumber on.

~Percy Bysshe Shelley

About The Author

Photo by Neale Eckstein

Jane Ross Fallon is an award-winning songwriter and performer. She holds degrees in English Literature and Composition, Music Theory and Performance from Eastern Oregon University, and a Master's in English Composition and Literature from Arizona State University. She taught English, Business Writing, and Public Speaking at Southern New Hampshire University for 25 years. In addition to this book, she has produced 6 CDs of original music and authored two other books with music:

Seven Songs in Seven Days, The Journey of An Arkansas Cowboy (2012)

Beyond Reason, Songwriting on Purpose, (2016)

For more about Jane, go to **http://www.janefallon.com**

Made in the USA
Columbia, SC
08 September 2019